CARLENE LOVE

Evernight Publishing

www.evernightpublishing.com

CARLENE LOVE

DEDICATION

For the plainclothes angels walking this earth, making others smile.

ACKNOWLEDGEMENTS

Dear Reader: Thank you for taking the time to read this story. I'm touched and honored. I would also like to thank Stacey Adderley for her constant support and patience. She is the publisher behind Evernight and she is a wonderful, inspiring woman I am happy to work with. This story ended up taking most of 2015 to write. That extra time was unplanned yet a true gift. The writing cave is a wonderful place, but the outside world is where inspiration lives and breathes. I've never learned so much than from having stepped outside. The biggest lesson? It's a little scary, but it's okay to be you—whoever that is. And it's okay to let others see.

Be you. Be here now. Do no harm.

Smile.

Live.

CARLENE LOVE

LET ME SEE

These Three Words, 2

Carlene Love

Copyright © 2016

"Patience is bitter, but its fruit is sweet."—Jean-Jacques
Rousseau

Chapter One

*The middle of June, Boulder City, Nevada. Or you
could also call it hell cuz it was so fricking hot.*

Clothes are really overrated, ya know. Oh, sorry, I
know this is just supposed to be that one line at the
beginning of the book that tells you the time of year and
setting. Let's just get to my story. Yeah, so here we go.
My name is Jay. I happen to be a stripper, which means
you're either blushing, giggling, checking your wallet for
ones and imagining my giant smile—come on now,
minds out of the gutter (insert that winky emoji girls are
so good at)—or super curious about what I look like
naked right about now. It's okay. I totally get that last
part. I'm curious about others in that way too.
You see, I'm just a guy who has no business
being in love with this beautiful angel who has me turned
upside down and inside out. She's all kinds of innocent.
At least she was. Before she met me. Hold on … I just

need a second. Sorry. And now, well now she won't even let me see her. Damn, I'm sorry. I've said way too much and this is a lot harder than I thought. I'm gonna do my best to piece this all together for you. Please bear with me. Can we just start this part again? Thank you. Sorry, I'm usually pretty funny but, I'm just not myself right now. I just want her to be okay. Ya know? If you're heartbroken or hurting out there, reading this, I want you to be okay too. Let's see if we can get through this together. So like I was saying, my name is Jay. I'm a stripper. And it's really hot here ...

****

The middle of June, Boulder City, Nevada ...

Jay hunched over and cupped the tiny white box mounted on his apartment's wall in his hands and hovered his thumb over the cooler button.

"Unhh," he moaned. "Thermostat, why darling love of my life? Why do you make me touch you so? I thought we talked about this. The hotter you let it get in here, the harder Daddy's gotta shake his ass to afford to keep it cool."

Sighing, he begrudgingly tapped the button one time and one time only, bringing the temperature setting down from 75 to 74. He let his forehead fall against the box and then petted it before pushing off from the wall and landing on the wall directly behind him. Yeah, his apartment was the small type. The hallway was what you'd call eency weency. What? He could say words like eency weency 'cause he had lots of other big stuff, you know, laying around here and there. Sometimes he cracked himself up, just not lately.

"Ahem. Hate to break up your little moment, but dude, you're so cheap! And on another note, it says it right here, and I quote, 'Someone who stealthily hunts or pursues another person'," D said, looking up from his smart phone, and eyeballed him like he'd just nailed something on the head with some serious hammering skills. If D really wanted to be useful, he could put some housekeeping skills to use and pick up all his crap from Jay's apartment floor. Jay kicked at a black shower shoe that caught air before it landed back on the worn, brown carpet right at D's feet. A second later, Jay had to duck or he'd have taken it right to the eyes.

And they couldn't have that.

"Hey! Watch the face!" he shouted at D, framing his face with his hands. "That's my paycheck you're tampering with."

His buddy broke out into an over the top laugh. Jay just stood there, waiting for D to sit upright again.

"Oh. My bad. You were serious," said D. "But come on, no one's looking at your face."

"Pssh. I have nice eyes. Like, twenty-five chicks told me so last night. You're such a dick."

"Yes, I have a nice dick. Why thank you, Jaymes, for pointing that out. Like, fifty women told me so this morning," D said before cracking up again.

"Oh, are we using full names today, Donovan? Don't make me use your middle name too."

A short and serious stare down ensued but quickly dulled back to harmless teasing a second later. They both knew who made their money being the pretty boy at work and it wasn't either of them. That honor belonged to their buddy Gabe. Even Jay could admit that Gabriel Medina took a good looking face to a whole nother level.

"Duly noted, silky," said Jay, referring to D's main crowd-pleaser which currently was so long it hung way past his shoulders. D pushed his hair behind both ears.

A new silver hoop caught Jay's eye. "New piercing?" he asked, looking at D's eyebrow and wincing. "Doesn't that hurt?"

D just shook his head like he'd been insulted. Oh yeah, Jay had to remember who he was talking to. Besides, it wasn't so much this eyebrow piercing that gave him sympathy pains, nor the two nipple rings, but the one he wished he hadn't seen one night in the dressing room. Jay grabbed his crotch in the kindest way possible and winced.

D cocked his head and blinked. "Pain only hurts if you let it."

"Touché," said Jay, realizing he'd just heard a part of his friend who rarely came out. He didn't even want to think about what the man might have gone through to have that as his personal motto. Jay wished he could move them past the awkward moment but true to his nature, D took it upon himself with lightning speed.

"Ah, don't pout. Everyone at the club wishes they had what you have, bro," he said.

"Maybe." But Jay seriously doubted that.

D gave Jay a "did you hit your head" look and said, "Maybe? Make a girl laugh and all the good looks and eight packs may as well pack it up and call it a night."

"Okay, great pep talk but we're starting to sound like girls." Even so, Jay was glad they'd had it, even if he'd never admit it out loud.

Shaking his head, he wondered if he should just go ahead and make it official and invite his buddy to room with him. It'd save them both money, a definite plus since they weren't exactly rolling in dough yet at the club. But then a funny vision of D the other night, making a giant pile of all his tips on the floor of their dressing room and then literally rolling around in it, made Jay grin.

But just that short consideration then had Jay shaking his head.

At some point, everyone needed to grow up.

After the craziness of the past few years and how hard he'd worked to get his life on track was starting to pay off, there were certain things he wanted now and a dude for a roommate wasn't one of them. Bachelor pads were overrated and smelly and while the average girl might not mind it much, deep down, Jay knew he wasn't after a girl who would settle for that kind of crap. Not anymore. He walked to his kitchen and pushed a disgusting chunk of soggy mystery food down into the drain then turned on the water and hit the disposal switch, which cranked to life with a loud grating sound.

"Oh geez!" he shouted as metal grinded against metal. Barely able to, he forced his hand down through the tight drain opening and fished out a few beer bottle caps. "Dude, really? Angry Orchard?" He showed Donovan.

"What? I like a fruity cider now and then."

"Bullshit. You like girls who like fruity cider. Don't let these end up in my drain again. They belong in the trash. Your trash. Kinda like how your hard cider lovers belong in your apartment. And, I am not hunting her," said Jay, shaking his head at the thought of bringing someone nice in here, prey or otherwise. "Just drop it and knock that ridonkulous Sherlock look off your face. You haven't solved anything, Holmes. I don't stalk women, they stalk me."

D's eyebrow hiked up giving him old man wrinkles on his twenty-something forehead while Jay tried to keep a serious face at how corny he'd just sounded.

"What?" dared Jay, his stoic face nearly cracking at D's wide eyes.

With his hands held palms up in front of him, D said, "Okay, Chuck Norris. Don't get your panties in a twist. *They* stalk *you*." He then grinned like he was glad to have the old Jay back.

Jay knew the real him was the one contemplating less one night stands and foolishly or not, a series of unforgettable, really long nights with *her*. The kind that would leave her curious for more time with him. Now if D was feeling concerned, he should probably be doing it over the fact Jay had these feelings for a nameless girl he'd yet to say a single word to who also happened to have a clingy, extremely cut boyfriend. Jay twisted his arm and flexed his triceps. He could compete. Oblivious to Jay's thoughts, D just shrugged and scooped up one of his dirty socks like it didn't matter a bit to him because he wouldn't be the one washing it anyways.

Nope, Donovan Roberts had girls who did that.

Jay probably could too, but did he really want to be nice to a chick just so she would do his laundry? Of course that's not how D would explain the help he got from his club regulars. He'd say they were just friends helping friends, a mutually beneficial arrangement. But Jay knew better. He'd been doing this long enough. Crazy how quickly you picked up on things in their business.

Male entertainer. Exotic dancer. Stripper.

Whatever you wanted to call it. It was a life lesson, that was for sure. But he liked most aspects of the job and that was why he'd stayed for so long. Some guys just handled it better and he was one of them. Didn't mean he wanted to do it forever though. He eyed Donovan, wondering about his friend's long-term goals and totally seeing him dancing until his legs gave out

from old age. Or his moneymaker shiny hair started
balding. Ew, not what he wanted to be envisioning. His
phone sounded from the counter just then, saving him.
Not for long though.

"Oh crap," he muttered, grabbing for it but
missing the call before it went to voicemail. D ignored
him for the time being. Jay checked to see that the call
had come from Mrs. Teague. "Damn." She afforded him
a ton of leeway, hell, she'd allowed him to fulfill his
mandated community service hours at the club on the
technicality that they were easily one of the most active
businesses when it came to supporting local charities.
The club sent dancers out to help host and run events at
least once a month and Jay had been at all of them. But
even Mrs. T had her limits. He'd check his time sheet
with Emma tonight at the club and call Mrs. T from there.
Yeah, she loved when he did that. Not. He'd yet to get
her to come down to see a performance. Clearly, she
would never be a regular. Too bad. Mrs. T could stand to
loosen up a bit. For an older lady, she was kinda hot.
Right in his wheelhouse.

Jay thought about things in the realm of mutually
beneficial arrangements and came to a surprising
conclusion. "You know, someone steady-ish might,
emphasis on *might*, be a nice change. She wouldn't have
to be my laundry maid, though. It's the 21st century,
dude. That is just wrong."

D's face twisted like he'd already moved on from
that convo and Jay was coming real close to sounding
like a loser.

"You say that now, but if she insisted, you
wouldn't argue. Trust me. You suck at household chores.
Don't hate the player," said D.

A quick look around the rest of his apartment by the both of them confirmed that. "Yeah, well you're no help."

D's eyes rolled wide and he said in his best hip-hop voice, "You should crack a window and air it out."

"None of the girls I've brought home have ever complained," Jay shot back, although D was dead on.

They looked at each other, apparently finding something amusing at the same time.

Jay pulled up his shirt and showcased his abs. D pulled his up, showing not just crazy mad abs but his dang nipple rings and Jay had to give it to him. "Dude, don't be such a showoff."

All kidding aside, admitting why no girls had ever complained about the mess brought Jay down.

He knew why.

They didn't care about those things as long as he took care of them in bed.

Up until the last few months, that had been a freaking balling, phenomenal lifestyle.

The million dollar question was why the hell he seemed so hell bent on wanting something different now.

It was really quite comical for a guy who was currently leading in the office pool for most souvenirs flung on stage. You hadn't lived until you'd been popped in the head or better yet, the junk, with someone's bedazzled cell phone.

Jay smiled.

The power of positivity.

He'd seen enough crap in his lifetime. Smiles and laughs were truly priceless and the female masses were drawn to him. There was power in what he was able to do for them and it would be hard to walk away from that. If there was one thing he had learned in his tenure as a dancer, though, it was that serious relationships rarely made it past first base in the club.

Emma and Sam came to mind.

Emma was still his manager but Sam, a great friend and the brunt of many of Jay's practical jokes, had quit dancing to be with her.

Could he do that for someone? Did he want to? Was there even someone out there who would be interested in a dude with his amount of baggage?

"Actually, yeah I think I have solved something." D reminded Jay of how annoying he'd just been with his whole dictionary stalker definition, thinking he knew something ... which he didn't.

"What are you talking about?" Jay asked D who just stood there busting through his phone, no doubt looking up crazy stuff while Jay downloaded the new routine music they had to rehearse for this week. Everyone was happy to have finally laid "Bump n Grind" to rest. God love Emma. Now if she'd just change the club name like she'd promised last year. The dancers had already been calling it S Club for like a year now. Club Mantasy got laughs out of people but the name didn't match the classiness of their shows.

"I finally figured out the answer to the age old question about the chicken and the egg," said D without looking up.

"Random much?"

"Always. Back to the chicken and the egg. Clearly, Jay Henriksen came first. King of them egg-laying chickens. Dude, you make me sad for mankind." D made the most annoying barnyard sound Jay had ever heard, even getting his head and neck into the action.

"Shut up," he said. "At least I don't look like some crazy ass rooster. You need a haircut," he said, referring to D's below the shoulders brown hair and the way it moved when D got into the rooster strut. "And what the hell? Sad for mankind? Dramatic much?" Jay pretended to toss hair from his shoulder like a diva, although his only came to his chin and was way too scraggly to do a proper flick like D.

But they both knew Donovan's hair really was his moneymaker and one of the reasons he'd been hired on at the club. The "long-haired, ripped, and could pass for Native dude" spot had been locked up tight the second D auditioned. Jay remembered how funny his moves had looked and chuckled to himself as he was prone to do when he pictured grown men doing the splits and getting stuck.

People didn't laugh enough these days.

It was a damn shame, he thought as he looked his friend over and appreciated the hilarity that usually ensued between them. As if on cue, D flicked his long girly locks. If Jay's living room had been full of horny co-eds, they'd have all gone on sex alert just then, desperately wanting D for one thing and one thing only.

Way too easy.

Too much power.

He couldn't feel sorry for the ladies though. It was rare that they really wanted to know what else the guys had going on. Like that half of them had degrees with some pretty heavy majors. They had second jobs and families they were helping support. Sam and Gabe had both served their country. Hell, they even had a serious writer in the bunch. Jay loved Julian's fantasy books and was really proud of him. He was proud of their whole group. Even Donovan Roberts, who was gonna eventually have to bite the bullet and face the fact that the adoration he got from the ladies wasn't based in reality. One of these days, D would have a choice to make.

Unlike Jay, he wasn't ready to do that yet, which was okay.

"I need lots of things." D waggled his eyebrows.

"A haircut is not one of them. Fool."

"Yeah, I know. You're right," said Jay while D ran his fingers through the length of his hair and pulled it back into a knot with the band he had around his wrist. Jay had to admit, it looked all right, he guessed. The women adored it so much so that D had been able to afford a trip home to Florida to visit his mom with the fruits of their affection, and that was all that needed to be said. Anyway, all Jay really wanted to do right now was prove to his friend how wrong he was about the finer point they'd just been debating.

Stalking someone implied he was obsessed and seriously looking. Oh. Damn.

"I'm not a stalker." He looked at his watch. "See, it's nine o'clock—" he started to say but it got him a giant smirk. "And, as I was saying, I'm not the one scouting chicks out the window right now. That would be you."

"Don't even try it. You know it's 9:07 and time for *her* to walk by and if I moved even an inch, your butt would be all up in here, trying to steal a glimpse." D made a disgusted face, which Jay knew was all for show, but looked downward toward the sidewalk below their apartments. "You even have me in on your stalking problem now. Bro, that is not cool. So when are you gonna man up and ask her out?"

"Maybe you should spend more time in your own window," Jay said, ignoring the uncomfortable, sincere tone D had just gotten in his voice. That was the second time now. Jay pointed in the direction of the pool where D lived in a unit just across the way. "You know it doesn't matter what time it is. If I wanted her, all I'd have to do is go down there and introduce myself."

"Right, so when's that gonna happen?" he asked, calling Jay out.

But the mere thought of actually doing that triggered some serious nausea. That was really odd. He tried to ignore the fact it had just happened. Women literally were on him five nights a week. Why did saying hello to this one in particular have him feeling like such an amateur?

D gave him another classic Donovan look that said Jay would be absolutely capable of turning on that kind of charm if it weren't for his severe case of chicken-shit-itis when it came to this particular girl.

She's too good for you, that's why. She won't want anything to do with a guy serving community service, who flunked out of college and who happens to be a stripper. Three strikes, you're so freaking out it ain't funny.

D whistled.

Ah hell.

Here we go.

"You're about to owe me for life, bro."

Did he even want to know? Yeah, all right that goofy look on Donovan's face could only mean one of two things. Either Miss Florida 2012 was standing on the sidewalk downstairs blowing obscene kisses up at the long-haired Cocoa Beach native or the big brown truck had pulled up and homeboy had a box of Whey Max hiked up on his shoulder, ready to deliver. Because no way would Donovan be inclined to whistle at Jay's girl. Not his type. At all. Way too goody two-shoes. Too off limits because the things Jay would do to D if he even thought about going there…

Wait, rewind. Your girl? Dude. Kool-Aid. Too much.

Jay rubbed his head for the thousandth time at the bat shit crazy stuff floating around inside it. He'd never even said hello to her!

Back to D's whistle. So which was it? Jay glanced at his watch again. It really was 9:07. Maybe it *was* his girl down there. Damn, maybe he *was* a stalker, but Jay wouldn't give D the satisfaction.

"Your future baby mama or Big Mike?" he asked. But if it *was* his girl, Jay wondered what she'd be wearing today and secretly bit his lip out of Donovan's view when he envisioned the smart green sporty top and yoga pants she'd worn the last time he'd seen her on her walk. They weren't at all tight but it didn't matter. Jay's imagination was strong enough to see past that *and* the big guy who was always with her. For the time being, he forced himself to stay where he was and not run to the window. Donovan grunted. What the hell was that about?

"Not *my* baby mama. Da-yamn. Your girl is lookin' hawt. And you're never gonna believe this, but she doesn't have that all-pro running back looking dude with her." D tapped on the window which made Jay nearly smack his hand from the glass. "Yeah, you keep standing over there with that 'I ain't a stalker' look on your face and you're gonna miss your chance."

D was always messing with him. Today must be no different.

She was always flanked by that guy who Jay was sure had played D-1 college ball. If that baller guy was his competition, there might not be a realistic chance to be had. Jay might not be her type. All the same, he admired that she was totally comfortable being with someone she liked, no matter what others might think. It was cool. Had to mean she had a solid grip on who she was because even in the year 2015, there were still people who had problems with biracial couples. He knew from personal experience. He was glad she seemed not to give a crap about that stupid stuff. He sure as hell didn't. Selfishly, he knew it was because of the hope it gave him. Maybe his job wouldn't offend her.

He'd stayed holding up his kitchen counter trying to play it cool for as long as he could. "Let me see," Jay said and practically shoved D from his spot at the window. Yeah, he knew he'd just proved D's damn point with that smooth move. Oh well.

"Oh," was all Jay could say when he saw her. Alone.

"Yeah. Oh," said his friend sarcastically. "You thought I was lying. So what was it you were saying? All you have to do is go down and introduce yourself?" D clucked like a dying chicken again.

"Bock, bock, bock!"

Jay should go.

This was a rare opportunity with her being by herself. Rare as in she never walked alone. Just look at the cute extra pep in her step as she went by. Her ass was amazing too, he thought, as he watched her do her thing and pictured them getting cozy by the pool at night, just the two of them.

Guilty.

Jay was a serious cuddler. He'd make her giggle when he dragged his fingers slowly up the outline of her hips, dipping down to her waist and back up to her shoulder and neck.

Damn, he was so attracted to her. Too attracted.

Not cool having that happen when the only other person in the room was D. Jay adjusted himself and used D's ugly mug to get some control back. But he still felt himself reacting to the excitement of seeing her. If D hadn't been around, he'd have just stood there and happily let her effects wash over him. It made him happy to see that someone could trigger his passion in that way. Sometimes he worried about becoming numb, being touched and pursued so much at his job. Now thoughts of her touching him burned like fire in his brain. His mind was sinking, about to picture her completely naked and walking slowly to his bedroom, giving him the privilege of watching her cheeks sway as she went.

"Mm, mm, mmm," he let out under his breath. Even though the view from behind was amazing, like always, he imagined a big smile on her face that matched this new joy in her stride and the long, black ponytail with extra bounce. Something had put the joy there and he had a sneaky suspicion it could be the fact she was enjoying some time alone since that was the glaring difference between today and every other day he'd watched her with that guy by her side. Maybe they were having problems. Maybe she needed a distraction.

It didn't feel great thinking of himself in that way but he'd been that before for girls.

His stomach did that weird queasy thing again and after rubbing it, he decided he wouldn't ruin her current bliss.

It's a good, solid reason not to go down there.

Yeah, no one would believe it but that really was important to him. Putting a smile on someone's face was pretty kick-ass but so was leaving well enough alone. If she was smiling right now, it was probably fricking beautiful and radiant, just like her walk. He would die for one glimpse of her eyes and imagined them being so beautiful they would drop a man to his knees, whatever the color, wouldn't matter.

Out of nowhere, Jay's mind slipped to Maggie.

It freaked him out if he was being honest and he jiggled his fists in his pockets trying to brush off the feeling of having thought about his sister just after lusting over this girl.

Mags looked nothing like her but had loved being outside, with or without people. Her smile had gotten him through so much crap.

Fucking cancer. He took out his fisted hand and rubbed it over his face.

Maggie would tsk at him until her face turned blue, but the thought of going down there and talking to this girl made him crap loads of nervous, which even D would say was just crazy. Damn, was he going to let this chance slip by? All he had to do was go down there and say hi. How hard was that?

"Knock, knock," said D. "Where is Jay-who-likes-to-get-laid? And … pausing for dramatic effect … she's gone," D said as she passed nearly out of sight. "You sick, man?"

Jay gritted his teeth and ignored D. Maybe he *was* sick. That could explain the gruesome ball of badness that continued to churn in his stomach.

"Not feelin' it today, bro. Wouldn't have been the right time to go down there. Let this girl enjoy her walk." Keep that pretty smile he'd imagined of hers.

He scrubbed his hands over his face again, completely shocked at his indecision, while D stared at him wide-eyed.

"Chuck Norris would go down there, ESPN dude by her side or not. Just sayin'."

For a second, Jay considered going after her.

A mouthful of hot breath shot from between his clenched teeth.

He just couldn't do it.

The truth as to why that was started pouring over him. She wouldn't be interested. That's how it always went down with the ones you liked too much. He'd made that mistake once before. Always better to just make a lighthearted joke about the heavy stuff and move on before it got you down or dumped and humiliated in public.

"Dude, I'm pretty sure I get more action than Chuck Norris and ESPN dude combined," he said to D, just trying to get him to lay off. If he pretended to be regular old Jay, maybe it would work. "She's just one girl on my street." Talking like an ass left him with a bitter taste in his mouth but the hell he was gonna sit here and get mushy with D. He grabbed at a bottle of water nearby and chugged it until it was empty. "Compared to the hundreds at the club. You do the math."

D made to fist bump Jay, apparently glad his friend was back, but as soon as their knuckles connected, D's face got all screwed up, like he had something to say. "You been to S Room with anyone lately?" D asked, uncharacteristically chewing at his lip.

Odd. Jay just gave him a chin nod. He had no intention of making good on any of the bs they were throwing around right now and talk about S Room was something the guys just didn't do. Usually. Jay couldn't shake the feeling D had something on his mind and didn't know how to just come out and say it. He gave D a few seconds to say more but his friend stayed quiet. Emma would freak out if she knew what still went on inside her brainchild meet 'n' greet room.

Occasionally, he amended.

Okay, guilty as charged. Jay was the one who kept the room secretly stocked with condoms, conveniently placed so Emma's prying eyes wouldn't see. Hey, it was just for fun and Jay figured it was more important that everyone be safe. Not a smart move to assume a private meet 'n' greet wasn't gonna occasionally end up in sex.

Maybe if someone had been looking out for his mom in that way instead of parenting with blinders on, she wouldn't have had Maggie at fourteen and Jay a year and a half later. Their lives could have been a whole lot easier had a child not been trying to raise two kids and failing miserably. Maybe Mags wouldn't have had to work crappy jobs with who knew what floating around in the air just to make her way and help him while he figured out his shit. 'Cause Mom hadn't stuck around to do it. He knew his resentment should be aimed at the cancer that had taken Mags and not their mom, but damn. The "what-ifs" never ceased to piss him off when he thought of her. But he knew that wasn't fair. Their mom had done her best. He wondered if she was enjoying life out in Arizona. The last Christmas card he'd sent had been returned.

Ack! He just wanted to get to work and ditch all these uncomfortable feelings popping up. Speaking of work, what would *she* think of S? Would it be too much? Make her tense up and wish she was somewhere else? Or would she find that she liked it? God, he wanted to know these things about her.

Her. Him.

Not there. You can't take a girl like her there.

Alone together but not in that room. Not at the club.

D may as well not even be in his apartment anymore. Jay's mind was in fantasy wasteland.

He'd make sure there was no one else around. Thoughts of them at the pool threatened to drown him. She would sit in one of the lounge chairs. Her long, black ponytail and those precision bangs would hang there, until he made them less precise. The things they could do together in the water and then out of the water once she felt comfortable with him and understood he'd shield her from everything except him. The laughs he could get out of her, the pleasure he could show her. Things he'd bet she didn't have a clue about, had never experienced, even with ESPN.

There was just something in the way she carried herself. Something about her energy that told him over and over again. She almost had this sheltered quality about her. Yes, he could tell just from the way she walked and carried herself. You could learn a lot about a person's arm swing if you paid close enough attention. Her arms. Pinned above her head in his hand while they lounged about by the water under the moon and stars. Frustration rained all over him because he plain and simply didn't know how to approach this girl.

Damn, he missed Maggie all the way to his bones. She would have had the answers. They'd talked about everything together. Even though she'd been so wrong about his worthiness, she'd been right about one thing. The mythical good girl she'd constantly told him was out there if he'd just take the time to look, actually was. Jay stared down at his feet. *Well Mags, you were half right. I looked and I'm pretty sure she exists.*

Jay shook his head and ran his hand up the back of his neck, feeling the hairs that tangled and curled back there when he sweated even a drop. He didn't even know how to do serious, let alone serious with a good girl. The part Mags had been wrong about, it was a huge part. Because looking at his reflection in the window right now, Jay didn't feel worthy. More like a coward afraid to go after the girl he liked and get shot down.

"Earth to Jay," said D. Concern marked his friend's face as the silver hoop rose with his eyebrow.

"Sorry man. I'm just out of it today."

D blew off the apology with a wave of his hand and a tightening of his ponytail. "I guess so. You actually let her walk right past you."

"I do that every day. Why stop now?" And then he said something that hit the nail on the head way harder and more accurately than D's whole stalker evaluation earlier. "Think about it, D. She's one of those good girls. She dates college jocks, not strippers." Jay looked at his watch. "Let's go. We're gonna be late for rehearsals."

With a rarely heard seriousness coming from his good friend, D said, "Don't sell yourself short, bro."

Funny, that was the same thing Maggie had told him the day she passed.

He kicked the thought to the curb before it made him feel even sadder. This was why he preferred fun over real. If it kept him single, there were worse things, right? But if that was true, why couldn't he stop thinking about the chance he'd just blown?

Hell if he knew.

Now he'd never know.

That girl is better off this way. You know it's true.

And with that, he grabbed his bag and he and Donovan left his apartment to head to rehearsal where he wouldn't think about good girls who were out of his league.

Before he ducked his head into D's old Camaro, he looked around, just in case, but she was long gone. He pulled the door closed hard.

Looked like his promise to Maggie was going to go unfulfilled. This weekend would be two years since she'd passed and he had yet to let anyone in.

Chapter Two

Kelley stole Anyell's workout playlist and downloaded it onto her phone. She put her earbuds into her ears and clicked play with a giant smile on her face.

Immediately, her hand flew to her mouth.

"Oh. My. God."

Man, she knew her brother's taste in music was more hardcore than hers, but holy cow.

It took a moment to adjust to T.I.'s word choices, but once she felt the heat on her ears dissipate, she closed her lids to bring her eyes back down to normal size and then slowly, let her head bob to the beat, finding she liked that part very much.

He'd kill her, Anyell, not T.I., if he knew she was listening to this stuff.

With an even huger grin, she patted her belt pouch, making sure her keys were secure, and then she left the house.

How had it taken her twenty-two years to get to this exact feeling? High school alone should have at least educated her on this rebellious high but it had somehow missed her. She supposed it could have something to do with keeping her nose cemented into the books and the rest of her body busy at any number of odd jobs. She didn't know what it was, but there was just something about this day. An unexplained energy poked at her, sending her skipping like a little kid again.

Warmth cascaded down her bare arms and then slowly hiked back up them as if it was deliciously out of breath from the long journey. The sun shined brightly in her section of Boulder City. It was a good thing she took after the cactus out in these parts because otherwise, the hot June day would have had her crying and miserable. As it was, she welcomed the sweat trickling down the middle of her back, and she was still standing in her home's doorway.

"Hello, sun," she said and bit her bottom lip, letting it eventually slide free beneath her teeth. "You look mighty handsome today and you feel extra good!" Okay, that may have been over-cheery but she couldn't help it. She considered for a second and then went ahead and tossed her yoga jacket she'd been holding, leaving it strung over her parent's couch. Anyell had suggested she wear it today even though she'd never worn it a day when they'd done their walks together. She'd told him she'd try but reminded him that heatstroke was worse than some random guy seeing her bare arms. She'd also thrown in a reminder that guys didn't look at her that way so he had nothing to worry about.

"Remember, high school? Remember, not a single boy ever asking me out and that lovely nickname, Smelly Kelley?" she'd told him last night while he packed for his very first business-ish trip. The insults and teasing over the way her clothes sometimes took on the odor of the restaurant kitchens she'd worked in had been hurtful and the reason why she kept so busy. That way she didn't have time to think about the mean things kids said to her. They hadn't been exactly kind to her brother either, assuming he was just a dumb jock. That's why she was so proud of his trip. Technically, Anyell was Cliff's associate, being his one and only employee, and what they were travelling to do was absolutely considered business. Anyhow, Anyell had relented but still told her of his preference that she be covered up.

"So protective," she said of her baby brother. "Let's do this." She closed the door behind her, wearing a very fitting green tank top instead of the boring loose ones she normally chose.

And with that, she was off and walking and letting out some very deep, perfect breaths.

This T.I. guy had a lot to say, most of it pretty, um, forward.

Kelley blushed, embarrassed that she still did that at her age, and imagined he must be very cute if his husky voice was any indication. Yeah, Anyell would never leave Boulder City again if he knew she'd found his jock jams. She loved Adele but seriously? This stuff was, how did the high schoolers she tutored say it? "On fleek?" And way better for fast-walking.

Kelley had one plan and that was to make the most of her three days of freedom.

Anyell might be younger than her but good luck convincing him of that. The boy would stroke out if she ever made time to actually get a boyfriend. The thought bothered her but she had priorities and work and school took up all her time. Still, she felt the loneliness and the curiosity all the same. You know what? Right now, at this very second, it didn't even matter that she didn't have a boyfriend. She had T.I., and, oh wow, she'd never heard *that* before. He could be her, what was it? Bae? See, volunteering to tutor for free hadn't been a total time-suck as Anyell had warned. Plus, three days of T.I. and Kelley would be the one impressing the kids the next time she saw them at the tutoring center. The Phillips had to be about more than making money, she frequently had to remind little brother, even though it mostly went in one ear and out the other. But Anyell was a typical hardworking guy who thought of little else than making money and taking care of business.

As she headed down the street, she tapped out a text to her brother.

Kelley: **Hey, Yell. Hope you find those parts you need. I'm going for our walk.**

It only took a second and she had a response.

Anyell: **Hey Kell stick to our route. Lookin now B careful Luv U**

Kelley: **Don't worry, I'll be fine. Love you too.**

There weren't many men in her life, but Anyell was the one she loved and respected most. He worked harder than anyone she knew and for only being twenty-one, had the confidence of an army of giants. What had he done when he didn't get into UNLV on a scholarship? Same thing as she had. Worked until he'd saved up enough money to pay for the first semester himself and then kept working. The two of them might be on the six year plan, but they'd eventually graduate college and make their parents proud. Anyell had given up football in order to do it and when everyone told him he'd never make it, that ball was the only thing he was good at and even at that, not good enough, he just quieted the noise and kept on. He even got flak from some people about working at the fiberglass shop for Cliff but it was a chance to learn how to run a business which was his end goal. She couldn't be more proud of Anyell. They were a universe of two. Even if he was ridiculously overprotective, she loved him. But she was darn appreciative of the trip he was currently on with his boss. She needed a break, like yesterday.

There went T.I. again, making her blush and putting an extra big shot of "Heck yeah, I'm listening to this! In public!" in her stride. Dare she say that was a bit of swagger she felt coming from her backside? Um, yes! Yes it was. And she liked it. A lot. Feeling untouchable, Kelley strutted up the sidewalk, giggling each time her ponytail swished across the bare skin of her neck, dumbfounded as to how she'd never insisted on this before. Anyell had to understand. What had happened to Mom—the date-rape she'd suffered as a young woman—

wasn't going to happen to her. She believed that with all her heart. It was time Yell realized he couldn't be her shield forever. Her life's dream was to be a teacher, but if she didn't get out there and live life, what lessons would she have to pass on? The simple answer was none.

Chapter Three

Jay stood apprehensively near his window, shading his eyes from the rays that made the leftover sweat on his chest shine. If the sun was already up, then he'd had a late night. Part of him didn't feel like he deserved to see *her* today but the other half knew he was too selfish to stay away. Not sure of the current time, he turned around and rested his back on the glass, thinking over his latest bad decision.

A few minutes later, that decision stumbled out from his room. As she passed by, collecting her things and not doing a very good job of it, he reached down and handed her a high heel that fell out of her grip.

For a second, he thought she was going to say something like, "Goodbye", or "Thanks, that was nice."

"Can you get the door?" she asked instead.

"Of course," he responded, not feeling much of anything this morning after their night of fun. It was wrong. He should feel something, right? *Sex is just sex,* he told himself as he watched her tiptoe her way to the door like she didn't want to step on his floor. Jay cringed then reached down and scooped up a random gathering of socks and shorts.

"Do you need help out to your car?" he asked after dropping the clothes on the couch.

She shook her head no.

That was it.

As fast as she'd come, she was gone.

Laying his palm flat against the door, he pushed it gently closed. Somewhere inside, he knew the young woman deserved more than what he'd just given her, whether she wanted it or not and even though she hadn't asked.

Jay rubbed his forehead. He went to his kitchen and stared at the top drawer. Letting out a breath, he took out a folded up piece of newspaper, needing to see the thing he'd placed inside but usually left alone. Opening it, he saw Maggie's face above a small paragraph, all in black and white print.

"What am I doing?" he asked his sister, wondering if somehow she could hear him.

His eyes teared up and he shouldn't have, but he read the obituary she'd actually insisted on writing herself before she passed. He got to the part that always formed a lump in his throat and an ache in his chest.

I am survived by my baby brother. I hope he sees what I see someday.

Because it would have been easy to sit there and just lose it, he carefully refolded the paper and placed it in the far corner of the drawer where it wouldn't be disturbed. Slowly, he pushed the drawer closed.

His fists burned to pound into the countertop.

This wasn't him. He was fun. He was lighthearted. He made people smile and laugh and reminded them to enjoy life. But, even his attempt at fun last night had left him feeling horrible this morning.

"What is there to see, Mags? I don't get it."

The brunette who had just left had gone so easily.

Without thinking, Jay went to his window on autopilot and stared out. Not a second later, she walked by, unknowingly lightening his uncharacteristic funk. He leaned in closer, trying to figure out why he was so drawn to her. A few seconds later, out of the blue, her head turned and she glanced up toward his apartment.

His breath caught. If the window had been open, he very likely could have fallen out of it as the whole of his body weight shifted and pressed against the glass. So strange, but the pull reminded him of magnets, like two parts unable to ignore the other. Was he just fooling himself though?

Shaken, he eased out of view, quickly enough so that he couldn't be seen but could still see out.

It was crazy, but his heart raced.

She'd never turned like that before. Not wanting to miss a second of his daily shot of whatever it was that she did to him, he was back at the glass. With her back to him again, she made her way up the sidewalk. He thanked the skies above for the perfectly placed traffic light that she didn't normally get stuck at. But today she stood there, a tap in her toe telling him she had energy to burn. He watched intently until she got the go to keep on with her trek.

Why did he do this to himself? Why did he want this girl to see him so badly? He realized he was never going to know unless he went down there and introduced himself.

Just then, as he was on the verge of going down and saying hi, his phone rang. Torn and with his eyes trained on *her,* he grabbed it from the top of a stack of fitness magazines on his coffee table. It was Emma. Personal calls were a rarity from his manager and so without hesitating, he pressed accept, all the while keeping his eye on *her.* God, it would be nice to know her name, he thought as the light turned green and she started to walk. Damn, maybe Em's timing was a sign.

"Hey, Hon. Good morning."

"Hey, Em. You too. What's up?" He was afraid he already knew if the other missed calls on his phone were any clue. While he probably could have gotten away with answering the phone during his time with the hot brunette, he wasn't a jerk and so he'd ignored the muted buzzing.

"I got a call a few minutes ago."

"Yeah?" Was this going where he thought it was? His own foot tapped as he watched the beautiful black ponytail bobbing getting smaller and smaller. *Damnit,* he mouthed.

"Special request for you, my dear."

Oh hell, that was not good. Emma didn't entertain special dance requests of her guys' time by club guests via phone like other places. Those types of meetings were always sorted out face-to-face so that the guy could decide for himself if he was comfortable with the girl or girls making the request. Talk about bad blind dates, multiply that by a thousand and you might understand. This was something else entirely. But, he'd made his bed and had always been the type of person to take responsibility for that.

By the tone in Em's voice, she was handling it like a real trooper.

"I'm sorry, Emma. I hate it that you get the calls when I don't answer them myself." It was his fault but a reminder that some greater force might be at work keeping him from making contact with his favorite walker. He watched the last bits of her pass out of view. Might as well deal with this now. Missing calls from his probation officer was never a good idea but like he'd mentioned before, Mrs. Teague tended to call when he was busy working. Or just plain busy.

"Give her a call. She just wanted to make sure you've been working the community service events and verify your volunteer hours. I told her you were my best guy for that stuff. You really are, you know. I don't know what I'd do without you to wrangle the guys. But you know that she has to physically speak with you and not just hear it from me."

Whereas in the beginning, he'd kept track of every second of his hours, he'd slacked off this past year, probably because he'd come to love the work and the people he worked with. "Emma, am I close?"

"Very. It looks like you should hit your mark after the next event. Then I'm going to insist you slow down. You've been at every single one. All I can say is thank you. I know it wasn't the best of circumstances that brought you to me and the club but I can't imagine a day of not seeing your smiling face. You give the place such a great energy."

Jay knew Emma and his former fellow dancer, Sam, had fought very hard to be together and Sam had lucked out hardcore. Emma was a keeper. Even though he would soon be able to cut back, Jay didn't mind donating his time. It was probably the one thing he did that made him feel remotely worthy of the way Maggie saw him, especially after the mess he'd gotten into that had earned him the 500 hours of community service. Plus, there was no greater high than seeing the smiles he brought to the elderly, the sick kids and the families taking home their rescue pets at the charity events.

"Oh, Em. You don't have to thank me. I'm lucky you keep me around."

"Jaymes Kerrigan Henriksen. Don't you even go there. I know you didn't deserve the crazy amount of hours the judge gave you—"

He had to stop her before she went any more Maggie on him, what with the full name and all. It was a good thing he enjoyed a good joke with the initials of J.K. Still, hearing the whole thing made him cringe. Why in the world his mom had gone to the trouble of thinking up such a complicated name for a kid she didn't really care about confused the hell out of him. All he really wanted was to be Jay.

"You know my position on that, Em. You do the crime, you do the time."

"Yeah, but we both know what you did wasn't really a *crime*."

That may be so but the university ethics committee had disagreed. Jay chewed at his lip and went to the kitchen, opening up his small pantry and grabbing the large tub of peanut butter and a spoon. He would ignore Em's last comment like he usually did. He'd take expulsion from UNLV and probation again in a heartbeat if it meant helping his sister. His only regret? That he hadn't written more of Mag's papers for her sooner.

The one thing she'd wanted more than anything else was to graduate college before she died. She hadn't even known he was doing it. But apparently it hadn't been so hard for her professors to put two and two together. How was a dying woman turning in massive, well-written research papers at the same time as she clung to life in a hospital bed? The one professor had been adamant that what Jay had done was tantamount to murder and had pressed and pressed until the ethics board handed down his sentence. In order to award Mags her posthumous degree, he had to complete 500 hours of community service. Hell yeah Jay got at least some satisfaction that he was doing it as a stripper. The narrow-minded old professor had to be hating that.

The second he finished his hours, he was marching down to the university ethics office and not leaving until he had a papered degree in hand with Margaret Lucille Henriksen's name on it.

"So hey, about the pool party bash, do you need me to take the lead on that?" Good, she wasn't responding back yet. That meant he'd told her enough times now that he would never publicly talk about his sentence and the circumstances of the case. There was no use. He was over that part of it and now, only focused on the results.

Emma sighed heavily enough that he heard her frustration with him. But fortunately, that's as far as she took it. "If you want to wrangle the guys for that, I'd love it. And hey, I happen to have someone interested in being your date if you haven't found anyone yet."

Oh no, not another one of Emma's famous hook ups. "Yes to organizing the guys for the pool party event. No offense and no thank you for the blind date. Em, I'm still recovering from the last one you set me up on. I don't know where you get these cousins." Not only that, he had someone in mind already. Just thinking of her calmed him. It was crazy. Made no sense. Two months of watching and he'd never even met her. The reasons mounted for finding out her name.

Just one more time, by herself. Please.

"All right, well if you change your mind…"

"You'll be the first to know. See ya tonight, Em."

They hung up.

Jay sank down onto his couch, contemplating Maggie's loss, Emma's offer and the possibility of *her*. With sweaty hands, Jay let his head fall back, closed his eyes and thought good and hard about opening himself and his world up to the possibilities. Maybe the asshole move to make here was the one where he let his sister's dying wish for him die too.

Tomorrow, he told himself. If she came back by tomorrow, unaccompanied, hell, maybe he'd see that as the sign. Maybe Maggie was up there trying to force a damn miracle his way. If she was, and her baby brother was ignoring that, she'd be all kinds of pissed at him. His eyes teared up and he let the spoon of peanut butter stick to his tongue.

"Mags, if this is your doing, make sure you're looking out for the girl." Because if he put himself out there and she actually liked him, and she got hurt because of it, that would be it. He'd be done once and for all.

Chapter Four

"Alone, again! Get yo ass outta this apartment, Jay!" D shouted at him.

A third straight day and still no boyfriend escort? At this point, he really was a straight up chicken if he didn't go say hi and he'd run out of reasons D would believe.

"I gotta go."

"Yes, you gotta. And you better go now. Lil Mama is stomping! Damn Jay, you might be too late. Something for sure has put a little some-somethin' in her step. Maybe All-Pro came back home last night and—"

"Shut up!" It could all be true what D just said but there was just something that told him she wasn't dating the jock. The body chemistry was all wrong and he knew a thing or two about body language. It was his job, after all, to be observant. Of course in his infatuation with the girl, he could also just be deluded. Right now, he didn't care. Seeing Maggie's message yesterday, dealing with the weird guilt he'd felt with his hook up and Em's blind date offer made him know he had to at least say hi to this one. As long as he was careful with her, he told himself, it would be okay. And, if for no other reason than to finally see what was up with the intense pull he felt toward her.

Jay snatched up his phone, his earbuds, his keys, and shoved as much as he could into his pants pockets. They sagged even more than usual but he didn't have time to change. "Dude, too much Adidas?"

D gave him the once over as Jay shoved his feet into his shoes. He'd tie them later. D laughed.

"Nah man, I mean Smurfs are cute and they do the head to toe blue thing. Plus she's obviously into athletes. If homeboy ever shows back up, someone's in trouble."

Jay glanced down at his shirt, pants and shoes, ignoring everything D said that was irrelevant. "You're calling me an Adidas Smurf? Damn."

"Yo, do you really have time to be worrying about that? Nerd."

Jay just flipped D off and ran out the front door, excitement and anxiety to meet the girl overriding everything else at the moment. As he raced down the complex stairs, he heard his friend call out, "Remember what I said the other day about you owing me. For life, bro. I'll be collecting starting tonight at work."

"Whatever," Jay hollered, on a mission and not looking back at D.

"Like I said, for life. And you're welcome."

Great. He didn't even want to think about the crazy crap D would have him do at the club. He'd been wing man before and it usually involved crossing lines even Jay'd rather not cross. But yeah, he owed D for basically being the kick he needed in his ass to get out there.

Jay busted out the complex's doors and onto the sidewalk below. He looked around and didn't see her right away. His phone dinged. It was a text from D who had the better view from two stories up.

D: **Top of hill just took a right. Headed 2 park.**
Jay: **tks**
D: **Go get her stalker.**
Jay: **fu**
D: **U wish. Unless I get special request 4 2 guys. Even then U wish.**

There weren't even words Jay could take the time to correctly text back so he just shoved his phone into his pocket and sped up the hill. He'd deal with D's blackmail tactics later. Because right now, all he knew was this woman who had hijacked his attention every day for the past couple of months was back. Alone. In pretty good shape because he had to be for work, he made it up the hill easily. Within a few minutes, he caught up and had her in his direct sights.

This is for you, Mags.

And then, *damn.*

She was even more freaking wonderful up close.

The months of catching glimpses of her through his second story window just didn't do her justice.

Jay slowed to a walk, leaving a good twenty yards between them. Yeah, he wanted a minute to take her in from behind but first did the smart thing and took a quick look around to make sure her escort hadn't decided to magically show up at the exact worst time. Nope, no escort. Just cars passing by on the streets and a few people geared up riding bikes.

He had just fallen under the spell of the back and forth swinging of her arms in perfect sync with her strides when she looked to her left. And then to her right. Good girl. She was practicing safety. Hell yeah, with a fine ass walk like that, and damn, her tank top hiked up in the back like she had it knotted in the front, she'd better be alert out here.

The pale skin at the small of her slender back left him in a daze for a moment…

"What was I thinking about?" he silently asked himself.

Oh yeah. Boulder City wasn't as crime riddled as its big sister, Vegas, but still. His chest tightened at the thought of her being hurt. He had no idea where the protective instinct came from and chalked it up to his love for women in general. Her efforts to remain alert made Jay happy inside and honestly grateful she'd at least been safe with that big guy by her side. He watched her ponytail sway from one pretty shoulder to the next and he licked his lips, wondering how her skin would taste. D's stalker comment made him grin. Guilty. But dang, look at her. Adorable? Confident? Full of life? Sexy? Hell yeah. All things Jay realized in that moment he wanted in a woman. This woman.

Should he let himself dip further into her? Could he really stop himself at this point?

A few sexy, black strands of her hair stuck to the back of her neck, curling up from her sweat and begging him to reach up and smooth them away. Higher up, the base of her ponytail was thick so he knew she had a ton of hair. It would feel amazing in his hands. Olive green must be her favorite color and the tight tank top her favorite new walking top. He was now a huge fan of both. *Would she date me? Would she want to be seen with me?* he thought as he looked himself over, remembering the preppy girl the other night who had launched into calling him ghetto trash when he refused to accept her drunken advances.

The club had its nights. And its gems.

She had to live close by, right? But for as much as he was always looking, he never saw her around the neighborhood. Yet another mystery about her he'd love to solve. The one place he'd definitely never seen her was the club.

For some reason, that thought left him with a smile more on the inside than out. He couldn't say why, he just knew she was innocent, something he didn't get the chance to be around much. As much as he didn't want to take that from her, he knew he needed to see it, hold it in his own two hands. To know that it existed in the world.

"God, I'd love to move with you," he whispered the secret to himself as he kept a far enough away pace with her. Walking, dancing, swimming, the type of movement didn't matter. He could just feel it in his bones that they'd make a perfect fit and have so much fun.

He didn't really swear all that much, but fuck. The thought of pressing up against her, taking care of her body and introducing her to his slowly and gently was sweet and hot and he did not need to be all strung up like that right now for their first meeting. 'Cause yeah, no way in hell was he letting the opportunity pass him by a third time.

"I gotta leave an impression."

He thought about it a few seconds, narrowing it down to two things: something subtle that would probably do the trick but might not leave her dying to talk to him again and then something that would definitely get her wondering about him but could also end in a slap.

Something about her, whether it was the way she carried herself all straight and proper, even when pounding the pavement, or the commitment she'd made to taking care of herself like this, was completely intoxicating and had him thinking all kinds of crazy stuff. Sure, she was a beauty, but he wanted to take her out. Her hands looked like they'd be so easy to hold. He was so curious about her that conversation would be plenty.

He shook his head at the thoughts she made him have. It was crazy.

Attraction was one thing. This had gone beyond that and he hadn't even seen her face, not really. A curiosity about how she'd look cracking up hysterically at one of his jokes nearly made him have to stop and go home to cool off and he remembered how the brunette the other night hadn't so much as giggled. Although to be fair, he hadn't been trying to get much out of her.

Laughter.

That was what turned him on the most.

He realized he was stalling.

He bit his bottom lip and told himself to speed the hell up. She was just a girl out for a walk. *Correction, a woman with gorgeous, creamy pale skin, bare arms, shoulders, and a neck you want to bite ... out for a walk. I bet she smells amazing.*

After one last appreciative glance at the backs of her knees where tight black leggings ended just above sexy heart-shaped calves, he manned up and sped up, a fairly simple task being that his stride was easily two strides longer than hers.

"Here goes something," he said, reminding himself that if he was gonna have to pay for it later at the hands of Donovan, he'd better make it worthwhile. No holds barred. This might be his one and only chance with her. He really hoped going with the second option didn't get him slapped. But something else told him even that would be better than letting her pass by and never knowing. Something about this woman called to him and it was time to find out what the heck it was.

Chapter Five

Kelley walked, breaking the rest of the rules Anyell had pounded into her head the night before he'd left. There were so many of them, she was just barely getting around to this latest onslaught. She felt absolutely fantastic about it and smiled. And then she took the end of her tank top in her hands and hiked it up before tying it in a knot. Be brave and live a little? Check and check.

She'd learned quickly from her newest boyfriend, The Weeknd—sorry T.I.—that there were just some songs that required her full attention. She'd heard his stuff on the radio and enjoyed the beats. But when she popped the earbuds in and listened to the uncensored stuff? Oh yeah. That was it. Most of it was explicit but some of it was just clever. He was just saying what lots of people probably thought but were too shy, like her, to voice out loud. Kelley was all about being real and true to oneself. Even though it made her stomach flip-flop, she was so about it in fact that she currently had "Where You Belong" on repeat and until she tired of it, that was how it would stay.

The freedom these past few days. To do what she wanted, how she wanted. Whether it was eating Twinkies out on the back porch and dancing around her parents' old patio furniture like a lunatic or refusing to lock the windows at night because she'd fallen in love with the doves cooing and the breeze carrying the distant, soft sounds of traffic to her hungry ears. How was she going to give that back up? Did she want to? Was it really asking that much to be let out of the house alone sometimes? Was it necessary they treat their home like a maximum security prison? Did Anyell really not trust her to look out for herself? Didn't he know she abhorred what had happened to Mom just the same as him? After all, she was the fruit of that horrible night their mother had endured whereas Anyell had been conceived on purpose and out of love, the only way Kelley would want it for him. If anyone had lived with the reminder their whole life, it had been Kelley.

But according to her brother, yeah, it was too much to ask. Which was why Anyell's phone call this morning saying he'd be home early tomorrow had her up and out extra early. She wasn't wasting one single second of this last day and only wished she'd have had the guts to plan something more spectacular than the simple morning walk. As it was, her plan for this last day was, well, spontaneity she guessed. Even if all she did was sit at the park all day and people watch. Okay, so that wasn't exactly the definition of being impulsive, but until tomorrow morning when Anyell was due back, she was for the last time, on her own. She wasn't even going to class today. An entire academic career that had shined since kindergarten would not be ruined in one day. Her four-point-oh would not be tarnished. She doubted very highly that the Nevada State university system would come crumbling down if Kelley Phillips took a Monday off to just, be free, one last time. It was summer break for most everyone else, for God's sake!

Kelley grinned as her favorite song started again. While he sang of confinement, she felt liberated. She was happily lost in this new boyfriend's "Oh yeah, yeahs" when she nearly had a heart attack!

Her steps took a stutter, she grabbed for her chest and her head shot to the right where a man she surely had never seen before walked right up beside her.

A blond, scraggly bearded man with personal space issues!

Her vision blurred from the bright sun but he was smiling? Hugely smiling?

What was wrong with him? Had he escaped prison? There was one not that far away in Jean. He definitely had the arms of an inmate with nothing to do but lift weights. She'd seen several episodes of "Sons of Anarchy" in her sociology class freshman year and this guy wasn't that far off.

Her breathing sped up.

Her first inclination was to hurt him somehow with whatever she had in her hands which was her phone. She could toss it and hit him square in the face because, because he was that close. She should do it. She should. Except he hadn't touched her. Not yet.

"Excuse me!" she said in as stern a voice as she could, gripping the phone tighter, ready to aim and launch it right between his eyes.

Before she could get herself to take the defensive action, he started motioning with his hands like he needed help. While keeping pace with her, he pointed to his earbuds which he pulled from his ears and then hiked his shoulders up and made like he was slashing his neck with his thumb.

Oh my God, he's going to kill me? In broad daylight?

She started to scream but the sheer look of panic that flashed across his face as she opened her mouth startled and stopped her. He showed her his earbud again, this time with more oomph and his eyes pleaded with her.

The earbuds were dead? Okay. Well that really sucked for him but that didn't excuse—

Oh! In the very next second he tugged her right earbud from her ear and put it in his left ear. What? She felt her mouth make the "w" and "h" but the word stayed lodged in her throat.

Her head swam at his weirdness.

Who in the world was this obtrusive and obtuse all in one?

Her mind clouded with the oddity of what was happening. So much so that she nearly exploded at him when he swung his left arm out right in front of her and she crashed into it. The second she hit him, her body's forward motion stopped. He quickly pointed to the car making a right hand turn into the middle school parking lot they happened to be passing.

"Oh," she mouthed, this time with a teaspoon of voice.

He nodded, smiled and then extended his right arm as if ushering her across the street.

Had she unknowingly taken drugs this morning? Maybe she'd mistakenly reached for Anyell's *vitamin* spiked juice rather than her plain old orange juice. Or maybe she was actually still at home in bed and dreaming.

No, that would mean she thought this strange man was dreamy.

Which she didn't.

He may have just saved her life but it was his fault she'd nearly died of a heart attack and then been so distracted that she could easily have just become someone's speed bump in the first place. Very much on purpose, she ignored the odd pull to turn her head and have a real look at him. His features, which she'd only seen for a split second, faded away until all she remembered was a gleaming white, toothy smile surrounded by the gangly stubble of a beard. Darn her body for apparently having imprinted the strength he'd demonstrated in that one arm when he'd stopped her. She cleared her throat and put more purpose in her step, questioning the thoughts of his smile and how she nearly gave her own smile in return.

Wrong, she thought loudly to herself.

Kelley gave a full look around to her surroundings. Plenty of summer school students and faculty walked the middle school campus and enough cars drove by on the streets to make her feel safe-ish. Maybe that was what let her decide to finally look back at him because it sure as heck wasn't that her heartbeat had calmed back down. No, that was still out of sorts.

She glanced his way and an immediate sense of calm washed over her.

So. Strange.

He still had that same smile planted firmly, firmly on his, um, his very kind looking face. She noticed he had his hands placed together and positioned over his chin and lips like he was praying. For what? That she wasn't about to scream bloody murder? She should.

Okay, and his beard wasn't the scraggly unattractive type she'd thought he had a minute ago. Looking at it now and feeling slightly less frazzled, she noted it was blond so it had appeared thin and sparse. But it was nicer, on this second view.

Slowly, her gaze slid up from his chin to his lips where she became momentary goo. Sneaking in a breath through her teeth, she saw that his lips were pursed like he was holding some big secret inside them. Of course he would have the cutest lopsided smirk going on because apparently the man upstairs wanted Kelley's run-in with this man to leave her tongue-tied. She'd paid attention to plenty of crush-worthy celebrities on screen over the years, but she'd never studied a man in this way. In person. So close. Kelley didn't dare stop at his perfectly strong male nose. No, just a few more centimeters upward and she made it to the most intimidating, daunting set of eyes she'd ever seen.

Seriously, did he realize how intense his stare was?

Did he always intrude on people this way?

He looked like the typical guys Anyell had told her to stay away from with his clear love for athletic wear and fit build to go with it. But, there was just something about him that refused to let her be so judgmental as Anyell would have been. The longer she gazed back into his eyes, the bouncier her heart became. What in the world was the organ doing in her chest? It was like the thing wanted out of her body so it could see the dazzling blue depths for itself.

Without a second's notice, she blurted out, "How old are you?"

"Oh, um, uh, yeah I'm 26," he stuttered out and then his mouth naturally seemed to go back to that grin that had her blushing. One corner looked like it was really pulling.

Twenty-six. Why in the world did I just ask him that? Ugh.

For a moment in time, they returned to staring into each other's eyes as she pondered certain things. It was then that she had her answer as to why she'd asked. With his hair pushed back from his face as if he'd let it dry that way after a shower, she could see the beginnings of lines and creases across his forehead and framing his eyes. He'd just told her he was 26 so he wasn't at all old. This made Kelley instantly curious to know if the lines were from smiling all the time or because he'd had a hard life. Anyell's eyes were actually the prettiest she'd ever seen and held something similar to this man's. Her brother had lived both a life full of love and smiles and also hardships. Maybe this stranger had too. Who in the world knew why she'd become so fascinated with him so quickly. She watched as his arm muscles flexed with just a simple movement and how nice his tan complimented them.

"How about you?" he asked, and it was as if they'd met hours ago, not seconds. It was like her asking him had been the most normal thing in the world.

"How about me what?" she said in return, not meaning to frown but doing it anyway.

Grinning, he said, "How old are you? Wait, let me guess."

They paused walking and then the most amazing thing happened. Okay, about five most amazing things. She may as well be an ice cream cone shivering like that, with the way he slowly looked her up and down from head to toe and back. Her second treat? He may have made an mmm noise. Might have. If not, she was making it part of the story anyway. But she was pretty sure he had. His fingers were no different than the rest of him because they reached out and touched her cheekbone without asking if it was okay. For the record, although it made no sense, it was okay. Four and five? His fingers rubbing across his own lips as he thought, and then, the wink. The wink! Who winked at her, ever? No one.

For a moment, she wondered if this was sheer desperation she was exhibiting. It didn't feel very good, if she was being honest. Too desperate. Too needy. Hanging on this stranger's every little notion the way she was? Probably not good.

But guess what? There was no helping it.

Nerves busted through the thin veil of coolness she had found and latched onto during his observation just now. "I'm twenty-two," she practically squawked.

"That's totally what I was going to guess," he said, his voice leaving her completely undone. "Your skin is really nice. And pardon me for saying it, but you have a rocking body."

Her brain, it was having a heart attack. A lump formed in her throat but didn't stop her next words. "Your voice is like a cupcake that's actually good for me."

What in the world did I just say? I am such a dork!

But amazing thing number six? His response.

"That is by far, the most freaking wonderful and fantastic thing anyone on this planet has ever said to me. But now you gotta tell me, what flavor?" His grin melted her worries away that she'd just gone complete freak show on him. He was totally okay with it? Maybe he really was a psychopath.

She began to shake her head no, trying to convey to him that she could no longer trust her mouth and the insane things that might fly out of it.

"Come on, pretty please?" he begged nicely. "Is it red velvet or birthday confetti?"

Oh boy. She thought about it, unbelieving she felt this comfortable around him so soon. Her eyelashes closed over her lids and when she opened them back up, she figured why not just say it. "Dark chocolate. Definitely."

Those words made him smile so big. And the laughter that came pouring out of his mouth wasn't the kind that others had done to her when they were poking fun and being mean. It was a joyous, hearty laughter, one she felt good about having caused. He ended the fit by giving her a very sly smile, like her answer had been seriously entertaining. If there was some secret, inside joke about dark chocolate, she wasn't aware of it.

"That was a really odd thing for me to say, wasn't it? I'm sorry. I have no idea where that even came from. I don't get out much. I mean I do. I actually attend UNLV. You'd just never know it. I'll be quiet now. I promise I'm not normally like this."

"No, no. I love chocolate too. Chocolate is great. The darker the better. I think you're adorable. You can just blame it on me. I have that effect on people sometimes. Plus, the way I just came up on you had to be startling. I just couldn't help myself. I had to meet you." He winked and smiled and then finished it off with another wonderful chuckle.

His reaction made her feel so good that she couldn't help laughing herself for a second.

Kelley was so glad she happened to look at his face just then and catch his expression. She had no idea what had caused it, surely not her… It was so overwhelming that she had to look away and catch her breath for a moment.

If he was stark raving mad, or a serial killer, he was a happy one. Being afraid of someone wearing that expression and now giving her the thumbs up would be like fearing a rambunctious puppy who was simply eager for a walk.

She had no idea what to do or say next, so Kelley decided to just keep walking for the time being and stick to the main streets.

He had to meet me? Had she heard that part correctly? No way.

She walked, attached by the ear to this happy, blond, stubbled man with a thing for athletic wear who was tall and excessively fit and … his laugh. She had to stop herself from telling him he had a laugh that was so wonderful it could light the Rockefeller Square Christmas tree, even in the dead of summer. His arms far outshone any other set of arms she'd personally seen. He was close-ish to her age. It took a moment to realize she was bullet-pointing all these considerations. Why was that again? Kelley decided it was best to turn back to face front and focus on getting in rhythm with him since she apparently was not. A skip step and it was better. Her bobbing and his bobbing were in sync enough for them to share the earbuds and not tug each other awkwardly. She wasn't short but neither was he.

"I'm going to be a teacher. Just, you know. That's what I'm going to be."

Oy! Again with the blurting. Why Kelley, why?

With her one free ear, she was sure she heard him cough and then chuckle. But then he spoke and Kelley was glad her new syndrome had at least garnered that much.

"A good teacher is worth their weight in gold. I bet you'll be great." His voice was so unique—deep and low like he meant everything he'd said but also flirty and light and with no accent she could discern—that she instantly fell back out of rhythm and had to skip step again. If he'd caught that, he was being kind and not reacting. His words embarrassed her but the more she listened, the more she liked.

A good teacher is worth their weight in gold, I bet you'll be great. She found herself repeating that, overwhelmed by his kindness and how articulate he'd just been and not wanting to lose the words. His words. She was so curious about him now, too, wondering what he did for a job, where he lived, if he had a girlfriend or a giant family he stayed with, if he'd gone to UNLV. There was just something so interesting about him and how he'd approached her and how they were having this conversation. *Where did you come from?* she asked herself as they walked.

"Oh, thank you," she remembered to say in response to his compliment.

Yet again, she couldn't help but glance his way and was delighted to find him looking forward. But from the side, she saw that he grinned sheepishly and it was then that she remembered who she had on repeat. Her head snapped back to face forward. Heat burned up her body as if she was no longer Kelley Phillips but rather a candle wick inside a barbecue grill.

This was impossible! If Anyell really wanted to protect her, he should have said how completely unnerving it was to be this close to a man. But she'd been around men, technically, her whole life, in school and now college. No professor she'd ever had or class mate or unrealized girlhood crush had ever made her feel this out of her mind, her skin, the realm of Earth. Just one more stolen sideways glance wouldn't make her a bad person, right? She turned her head toward her … companion … and just when Mr. Weeknd sang about leaving a mark, she astutely locked her jaw back to face forward and tried not to die of embarrassment. Straining her eyes as hard as she could to see him in her peripheral without giving it away, Kelley caught him lip synching perfectly.

There was no missing him mouthing the words to "Where You Belong".

She swallowed, glad the song quickly came to an end after that.

Oh crud! But there it went starting up again and in a not so smooth look to her right, this time she saw him mostly straight faced except for that dimple-tipped smirk of his. Other than that, he just kept walking and looking ahead.

Kelley tried to play it off and managed to maneuver the buttons of her iPhone to the playlist and took the song off repeat, allowing the rest of her "Edgy Walk" playlist to forge on.

Yeah, that was cool except for the first lines Katy Perry sang were about a certain colorful and proud bird she had every intention on seeing. Kelley's eyes popped so wide she was sure they'd never go back to normal size. A headache began to set in. Oh dear God, please don't let him be mortified. Yes, in a strange turn of events, she was the one feeling bad for this stranger. Quickly, she fumbled around, worse this time because trying to get the phone to wake back up and get her to the playlist again was like being stuck in a nightmare where you were trying to dial a phone number because your life depended on it and you couldn't get the numbers right and Freddie was on your tail the whole time. Basically you were bad guy dead meat.

Finally, just as Katy serenaded them about what a sight his *architecture* was, Kelley successfully hit the next button. She let a straight-mouthed and apologetic smile slip out for his benefit. In case he was looking, which he probably was not. Oh thank heaven for Rihanna. Finally, a song with the perfect beat to propel them up the next hill and nothing about seeing private parts and being liberated. Kelley couldn't decide if she owed Anyell his favorite home-cooked meal when he got home or a nice long Grey's Anatomy marathon, her favorite show since the age of twelve. Was she appreciative or upset that he'd known exactly what he was talking about?

Smart girls like you belong in class. The world is a messed up place, Kelley. You don't want any part of it and I promised Mom and Dad I'd always look out for you.

They may have been pieced together as a family, but a day didn't go by when she wasn't thankful they were hers. Anyell's father was the love of her mom's life and the only dad she'd ever known. She hoped their parents were out enjoying their retirement. They'd earned it. A nice, unadulterated breath cleansed her entire being in that second. She knew her brother only meant well. And while she wouldn't call this current situation dangerous, it was definitely out of the norm. But for as much as she loved knowing she had Anyell looking out for her, it was time Kelley started finding her own way. Out from under his watchful eye and the promises he'd made to Mom and Dad who were following a lifelong dream of RVing across the country. If she ever wanted something like that, she had to assert herself and grab life by—she giggled—by the earbuds.

Finally, as she walked, remembering the potential each person had inside them to make the world wonderful, she took that warmth generating inside her heart and smiled a small smile at the treat the universe had given her just now. How silly to think she had anything to fear about this guy. Clearly, he was harmless. Maybe he had an overprotective big sister at home and this was his first chance to get outside on his own too. Maybe that explained his lack of social skills. She wouldn't be surprised if he'd rarely been around people with as awkward as he'd been coming up to her. Sweet though, she thought. Amazingly, the next song was another tame one. And the one after that.

It dawned on Kelley that they hadn't spoken to each other in so many minutes, aside from him mouthing the words to every song pretty much perfectly. Their communication had gone radio silent. Probably due to her chocolate cupcake brilliance. Unless you counted the telling way in which she kept stealing sideways glances although she was gonna have to knock that off because she'd already nearly crossed the street in front of a car, tripped on a jagged portion of the sidewalk and her eyeballs were feeling the strain at this point.

She wasn't keeping track of the time, but with the number of songs that had played, they had to have been at this awkward walk for at least a good twenty minutes. Maybe more. Now that she didn't feel like she was about to be stuffed into the trunk of a car, Kelley's mind eased into more rational curiosities. Just the basics. What was his name? Where had he come from? Why had she never seen him before? The biggie, why in the world, out of all the people outside today, had he picked her to, well, whatever it was he'd just done? Share earbuds with? Man, she reminded herself how strange this all was.

Just then he scooted into her in order to avoid a mother being tugged by an anxious dog and toddler combo. She felt the contact everywhere. Her skin was hot before it cooled back down to just warm again, separating from where their arms had just touched. Looking down at her forearm, she saw them. He'd just given her goose bumps. And it was the dead of summer so she couldn't pretend it was from the cold.

Oh geez, really? Dear God, please don't let him be seeing this.

But of course, he looked down just at that exact moment. What he did in the next second completely mystified her. Before she knew it, he took her right wrist into his left hand and reached over with his right hand to rub away the chills. All as they walked without missing a beat. His rhythm was amazing. And extremely, could she admit it? Extremely … sexy. She bet he could dance with his knowledge of music and without thinking, she bit her lip as she pictured him moving on a dancefloor somewhere.

This had just gotten real. Sorry T.I. and The Weeknd.

Kelley swallowed.

She'd never swallowed this much. But as mind-blown as she was with how her morning was going, she also felt lost as anyone could possibly be. This sort of thing *never* happened to her. Her whole life, she'd been handed from one protector to another and while grateful, Kelley just wanted to breathe. On her own. For once. To make her own decisions. Her own choices.

For goodness sake, what was this all about if it wasn't one of those signs she'd read about in her modern ideas class? She'd be crazy to ignore that, right? But just as she was thinking that, her playlist officially came to an end and since she'd turned the repeat function off, all they heard for the next few steps was silence.

It was then that he took her phone from her and began typing in her passcode. Dang, he was observant and gave her what looked like an apologetic look. Anyell would hang her for letting that happen and yeah, Kelley wasn't very proud of herself in that moment either. He actually wagged his finger at her, just like Yell would have done. The message was loud and clear. Be more careful. Shield your keypad the next time you decide to type your passcode into your phone a gazillion times to keep someone from hearing all your secret smutty walking music.

The next thing she saw him do was navigate to send a text but she did not recognize the number he tapped in. She wondered who he was texting with her phone, maybe a ride for himself? The more she stared at him and saw past the wildness of his features, she saw how truly handsome he was. The second she wondered if the text could have been for a girlfriend, she felt her heart sadden. Silly, she knew, but he was just so charming, in his own weird way. How could he not have someone? For the first time, their pace slowed. Squinting so she could see every letter, she read as his message came up on her screen in a blue conversation bubble signifying it had been sent by her own phone: **Hi TY btw Jay**

Jay.

It was a nice name and fit him well, she thought, mentally repeating it a few eighty more times.

Unsure of exactly when it had happened, she'd somehow gotten past his forwardness. He didn't have a bad vibe to give off from what she could sense. Granted, her sensing skills were severely under practiced but if he was bad, she'd have known, right? Her gut wouldn't just fail her like that. Of that, she was sure.

She made sure to smile at him. Nothing huge and goofy like what she felt inside but something that echoed the thank you he'd just abbreviated for her in his message. She went to retrieve the phone from him but apparently he wasn't done and he continued holding it firmly in his hand, just out of her reach. He shot her a wink that made her insides tumble.

He made his way back to her playlist, this time hiding the screen from her by tilting it just enough. If he made a selection, he must have also tapped the pause button because it stayed quiet. Keeping her phone in his hands and hidden, he pulled the earbud from his ear and replaced it into hers. She wasn't even grossed out, not by a long shot. His fingers tickled the sensitive skin of her ears and oh heck, if she didn't get a fresh wave of goose bumps. How embarrassing.

He looked up and gave her a huge grin. If he'd noticed, and he probably had, he was at least being a gentleman and not busting her out about it. He then nodded with his chin that they had come nearly full circle around the giant block and were back near the intersection where he'd first given her the heart attack. With a warm hand that gave her a third set of shivers, he handed her phone back to her and then without any warning, placed a kiss on her cheek. Then, with another wink, he jogged off in the direction behind her, backtracking.

Wait, what? Where was he going?

Not ready for him to just be gone ... to just poof and disappear into thin air, she couldn't tear her eyes away from him or her hand from her cheek.

He didn't even know.

That had been her first kiss.

She stood there at the light, in beautiful shock, not crossing the street for fear of losing sight of her mystery man and waking up from this dream. This dream with *Jay*, she corrected.

At the point where cars began ignoring whether she intended to cross the street or not and went on their way without even pausing in the turn lane for her, she finally lost sight of him. Kelley didn't realize she'd been holding her breath that whole time. A wave of lightheadedness came over her and she leaned against the traffic light pole for support.

"Oh!" she remembered the song he'd selected and left on pause for her. Excitement to find out what it was had her heart beating like a little kid on a trampoline. Wanting to keep it a surprise until she was safely across the street where she could sit and listen, she held the phone to her chest and then crossed, making her way to a section of raised curb where she sat and woke up her phone. She tapped in her security code and saw the last song in the world she'd ever have thought anyone, especially a man as perfectly odd and funny and yes, handsome, as Jay, would have selected for her. Her cheeks burst into a red joy, in sync with the fluttering of her heart. Of all the songs he could have picked, he chose this one. The one she secretly listened to every day and night, dreaming of and wondering about things that until about five minutes ago, had never before happened…

****

Jay was nearly out of breath as he finally made it back to his complex entrance. Well, he'd done his best. By virtue of texting technology, they had each other's numbers now. He pulled out his phone and brought up the text he'd sent himself from her phone and edited to add her name, which damn, he hadn't gotten.

"I'm such an idiot!" he screamed, scaring Mrs. Silver as she escorted her two boys and an assortment of aqua-noodles to the pool. "Sorry," he mouthed as she smiled, forgiving him. She was a nice neighbor.

He thought for a second and then typed the first thing that came to mind when he thought of *her* in the contact section:

"A-N-G-E-L"

"Angel." He said it and smiled, hoping she wasn't having second thoughts and using his brilliant move to hand over his name and number in a police report.

But no, she was down with it. He could tell she'd been into him when she let him rub some ridiculously cute goosebumps from her arm. That thought alone had him closing his eyes and fantasizing his way through dinner, dancing and if he was lucky, an entire night full of laughs. And the pool! If she let him touch her skin again, he wouldn't stop at dedicating a song. He'd take as much as she was willing to give, which he knew was something. He'd caught her looking at him and while she hadn't given much away, there had been just enough in her embarrassed smiles.

That made him wonder what she thought of the song he'd picked for her from her playlist. He'd searched so quickly and they were all fast songs, so it could have been the worst pick he'd ever made, but there was just something about Rihanna's "Where Have You Been?" that seemed appropriate.

Jay made his way inside his complex doors and up the two flights of stairs to his apartment. Once inside, he saw that D must have hung around for their favorite chocolatey peanut buttery delivery and then helped himself to a box of the protein bars. That was cool. Jay would mess with him later when they met up and claim the missing box was payment for the favor of kicking his ass to go meet Miss Angel. Jay let a huge grin loose. Man, he was fricking excited and bounced around his apartment, gathering his stuff. He couldn't remember the last time he'd felt this fantastic.

Hungry from the extra adrenaline, he munched a protein bar and glanced at his watch. It was still early and like most days, today was a busy one. While the walk had been stimulating as hell, it was nowhere near the level of cardio he needed to stay in dancer shape so Jay grabbed and packed his bag and then headed to the gym where he'd undoubtedly see most, if not all, the guys he worked with at the club. After that it was community service time at the local senior citizen's home, then dance rehearsals, and then work. He probably wouldn't roll back home until one or two tomorrow morning at the earliest.

The schedule didn't bother him. It kept him out of trouble if nothing else and he liked visiting with the grandmas and grandpas. But damn, the one thing it didn't give him was time to take Miss Angel out on a proper date. If he wanted to see her again today—which damn straight, he did—he'd have to invite her to either the retirement home or the club.

It would surprise most people, but he preferred the first. As much as he'd have loved to show off for her, he just wasn't ready for the whole "I strip for a living" reveal followed by her inevitably walking away.

He pulled up to the gym, parked, and prepared to send her a text, unable to stop thoughts of opportunities for them to be alone and empty rooms at the convalescent center. He could show her a private body roll. Damn, maybe even teach her how to do one. That would be hilarious. And fun. He'd never insist on getting that far that fast with someone as shy as her, but thinking about it felt amazing.

"Here goes another something. Don't let me down, Miss A."

In his blue convo bubble, he mouthed out loud as he typed: **Where R U? Winky face. I know where U should B. Come see me. Noon. Bridgeway Retirement Village.**

So, that was the unsexiest text he'd ever sent out and nearly laughed at it.

He stared at the message and waited a few seconds, hoping for that instant reply. It didn't come and he let a few more seconds stretch into a few minutes. He had to get inside and get to working out. There was one mess of black hair, one beautiful womanly walk and one perfect, gorgeous smile he'd be doing it for. He hoped like hell she showed up. The grind was finally getting to him and at his age, Jay was feeling less of the fun in the long nights of partying and more of the loneliness. But not tonight, not right now. Right now all he could feel was his stomach twisting with hope that she'd show up for him.

First, he sent out another text: **PS what's your name, angel?**

An uneasy feeling washed over him when she again didn't text back. Had he been totally wrong about their connection? Had he overdone it and scared the hell out of her? Had she somehow recognized his face from club advertisements all around town and just been kind not to let him know he wasn't her type while they'd walked? It sure had felt right, hanging with her. S fun and easy. He stuffed his phone in his pocket for quick access if she did reply and got his ass to the gym.

****

Donovan had expected a bigger smile to be plastered on his friend's face but what he saw was more of a worried and trying-to-blow-it-off mix.

See, he paid attention.

Sometimes.

Anyway, it took a minute, but Jay finally set his phone down, leaving it on the weight bench to go to the bathroom. Quickly, and only because he wanted to make sure Jay hadn't chickened out again, he easily maneuvered through Jay's passcode to get to his messages. He opened up and found exactly what he was looking for. Except for it was all wrong. Homeboy had asked the girl, whose name had to be Angel, to meet him at the old folks' home. Dude, seriously. Chuck Norris would not approve. No way should his friend get lucky at that place.

He knew Jay would be pissed at first, but he'd get over it and thank D later.

Donovan opened up the message and sent a new one to Angel. Nice name, he thought as he typed: **Hey Angel, change of plans. Come c me at the club 2night.** And then feeling extra helpful, D added: **I'd love to dance for you. Addy is 877 Nevada Way.** He hit send just in time to maneuver the phone back to Jay's workout playlist and lay the phone back down on the weight bench. Donovan played it off like he'd just come from getting a fresh towel to wipe down some equipment.

He just smiled and went back to his business. Jay wouldn't owe him anything for this. He loved that dude like a brother. The guy deserved to be happy.

Chapter Six

This time, she would be smart. Even though her lack of safety protocol had landed her the most interesting morning of her life ... how many times had she re-run the entire walk and how much more adorable and handsome had *Jay* become with each pass?

"The man can wear the heck out of some track pants," she said, tightening her ponytail high on her head. She then shook her head, not understanding even a tiny bit of what was going on between them. In reality, it was probably much less than what she thought. But then unable to help herself, she wandered off to dreamland.

It was his smile that had basically enslaved her at this point. She sighed and then smiled a private yet completely telling smile. If Anyell had been home, she'd be caught.

She wouldn't change the crazy morning walk for a thing, but she did appreciate the fact that she was a single girl alone and going out at night was new for her.

His texts! He'd invited her out and she'd spent the next couple hours freaking out with no idea what to say in response.

Yes, first to a retirement home, which she actually thought was kind of adorable. But then the dancing thing. The dancing thing! She'd finally texted him back, although it had taken her forever to compose her reply, including several, okay, about fifty starts and erasures and new starts. The great hope had been for a mix of smart and sophisticated, but it ended up being short and simple: **See you tonight.**

Kelley had no idea if she'd said the right thing or too much or not enough, having never done anything like this before. She read the three words over and over until she finally decided she was being silly and not to mention, obsessive. She felt like such an idiot.

You're just new to this, is all. Don't beat yourself up.

That was a good point and he'd been forgiving of her inexperience thus far with the awkward blurts and all. *Cupcakes, anyone? Nerd!* Kelley couldn't help but think more and more how his own oddities mixed with hers had made for one pretty nice, albeit goofy vibe.

Still, blood rushed to her heart and crept up in a warm, pink cloud over her collar bone, neck, ears, and face as she stood at the mirror and fixed her bangs for the five thousandth time. The text invitation to come see him dance had nearly knocked her off her feet. It was as if he'd read her mind and seen her curious fantasizing about his moves. Of course, the first thing she did was search the address online, you know, just because a girl couldn't be too careful. CSI had at least taught her that.

Mr. Jay was apparently an exotic dancer at Boulder City's only, um, well she guessed it was a strip club. She had to admit, the thought of going there made her want to throw up. No way was she cut out for that kind of scene. Everyone there would be beautiful and sexy and beyond cool and she would look like a turnip or some other really obscure garden vegetable. Plain and boring.

But Jay? She didn't really know him, but the allure of a place like that seemed to both fit him perfectly and yet not at all. No wonder he oozed charm like marshmallow sugar coating.

The whole thing with Anyell being out of town and Jay blasting into her world this morning were all the motivation Kelley needed to swallow the nerves and fit into her best dress. She'd worn it out one other time for dancing but wedding dancing and the bride's lonely cousin as her date paled in comparison to where she was going tonight, at his invitation no less!

"God, I hope he likes me in this." She smiled largely and inspected her teeth in the mirror, licking over the tops. Giving in to her nerves, she went ahead and brushed one last time, finding some relief in the minty aftertaste having killed any remnant of the tuna sandwich she'd scarfed down for dinner tonight.

She'd never had the chance nor need to be pretty for anyone but in the blink of an eye, it seemed, that had all changed. She wanted him to see her. The real her, not the mouse everyone thought she was. The real and whole woman inside who was intelligent and caring and yes, the one who yearned for fun.

A thirty minute walk had let her know that Jay oozed fun.

It felt so ridiculous, but she let herself have the thought anyway. One of these days, she'd have such a great story to tell about how they'd met.

"Okay, now you're just getting way too far ahead of yourself," she said and bit half of her bottom lip and smiled in the mirror and continued getting ready for her night.

Kelley gave a final series of swipes. One to her bangs, one with her lip gloss, and one of lotion over her bare arms. She tugged down on the shiny gray, knee length, sleeveless dress, still unsure she could pull this night off, and stepped into her pumps. She wobbled at the ankles but righted herself, holding onto the wall for support. She absolutely could not wait to see Jay.

Oh, and the part about being smart this time. Just in case something happened, she jotted a quick note to Anyell that she was going out dancing with a friend to a place on Nevada Way, and that he should not worry about her. She ended it with a heartfelt, "Love you, Kell."

And that was it. Kelley Lorraine Phillips, Language Arts major and junior high teacher in the making, was stepping out to have a night of adventure, because what was the worst that could happen? She started mumbling a list as she walked to the front door.

"He could change his mind, he could ignore you, or you could be a disappointment once he sees you in his elements and realizes what a giant oddball you are." But she knew the worst one had yet to fall from her lips. She went ahead and stated it out loud to take away its power. "You chickening out and not having the guts to show up, Kell, that is the worst thing that could happen. So get your butt in the car!"

Under the glare of the motion sensor lights lining the front porch of her parents' home, she got into her hand-me-down student car and turned the key in the ignition. It started up after two tries, just like always. She drove, listening intently to the voice of her phone's navigation, trying not to psyche herself out and turn around like a coward and scurry home.

"This is going to be fun. I can do this."

Most importantly, someone made of flesh and bone was expecting her.

Her hand drifted from the steering wheel and settled over her parted lips as she realized something for the first time. She wasn't just going to see Jay dance. Not at a club like that. There would be more. More than she'd ever seen before. And to be honest, there was a great possibility she wouldn't know how to handle it. She prayed for a straight face and no, or at least minimum, blushing. A definite thrill ran up her insides. God, and how quickly he'd gone from mad and scraggly to cute and scruffy. But the thought of seeing him strip down, in a room she imagined would be full of beautiful women, overwhelmed her like nothing else. As free as she'd been these past couple days, she could never imagine herself doing anything like that, not even if her life depended on it.

It was pitch black out as she drove but the city lights at night were so beautiful in person, and the moon hanging over everything ... so much better than on the TV.

"In one mile, turn left onto Neh-vah-dah Way. The destination will be on the right," her phone chimed. She squirmed in her seat, feeling more and more of the excitement as wild and foreign thoughts of being Jay's guest began to rule her body.

At about the same time as she started wondering how much dancing Jay did in comparison to the stripping part, Kelley's car made a wretched sound. Like a metal belch.

"No, no, no. What? Come on, old girl. Not right now," she said and luckily pulled over to the side with the last lurches the Pontiac had left in it. She tried several times to get the engine to start back up but to no avail. Plain and simple, the thing was dead. Finito.

"Crud."

She tried all the tricks Anyell had taught her but nothing worked. Her ride was done for. She could call a cab but the club's website said there were two shows and the first one started at eight. It wasn't like she had money to waste on a fare and Kelley didn't want to miss the show. She felt fairly confident in her ability to walk one simple mile. Still sitting in her car, she switched the driving directions to walking directions and eyeballed the route which looked pretty easy. She had two long sections of street to walk but felt she'd be fine.

"Here we go. The things girls do for cute boys," she muttered and smiled, appreciative for the cute boy who had her out doing this. Jay was one of the cutest, she'd decided on the drive over. And so sweet. Yeah, she wouldn't kid herself. She liked those things about him but the thought of watching him dance—exotically—was a mind explosion in itself.

On the thrilling high of that, she quickly tapped out a text to him: **Almost there.**

One mile should take her fifteen minutes tops and that was accounting for the heels and sexy dress. It was June so she hadn't brought a sweater to cover up with but the club was so close and the temperature couldn't have fallen below the seventies yet.

"You'll be fine. It's Boulder City for heaven's sake. Just get to walking," she told herself, smartly glancing right and left and then behind her, the dark admittedly making her nervous.

Nothing good happens after midnight but it's barely 7:30. You're fine.

It was when she had half a mile to go that she knew she'd made the biggest mistake of her life. Her gut didn't fail her this time when she saw the three men hanging out on the street and in an instant, felt the cold trickle of ice race up her spine to her skull. She'd never felt this before, but something deep inside screamed at her.

Run Kelley. Just run.
She did, but so did they.

****

Jay was not in the mood for their pranks tonight.

And if he didn't murder Donovan, it would be a miracle. D never should have invited Angel to the club tonight. But ever since Jay had found out that's what he'd done, he'd been stalking his phone for a reply from her.

"Dude, where is my phone?" he demanded of the guys standing around back stage with him. "Gabe?" he questioned the only one of them who would own up to having hidden it. But all Gabe gave him was a shrug. "You guys suck," he said and continued searching through his bag.

Finally, with less than five minutes to go before show time, Gabe walked back by and tossed the white and blue contraption his way. "Found this in the sock bin. You might need to sanitize it," said Gabe, wiping his fingers on his suit and tie costume.

The sock bin was where all their smaller costume parts got tossed by the stage manager and when Gabe said socks, he didn't mean the kind that went on your feet. Although he was peeved that he'd been on the receiving end of a prank, Jay was just glad he had his phone back.

"Thanks man," he told Gabe who held up three fingers, signaling the amount of time they had until they went on. Jay nodded and Gabe turned away from him and began rolling and stretching his neck.

Quickly, Jay woke up his phone. "Yes," he silently said. There was a notification that he had a message. He knew without a doubt it would be from her and tapped the heck out of it to open its contents: **Almost there.**

At first, he blew out a breath of relief. On second glance however, he saw something that didn't sit well. That had been half an hour ago. Boulder City was not a big town, you could get from one end to the other in five minutes if you drove like Jay. Maybe she was the type who said almost there as they were stepping into the shower. His mom had always been like that. He couldn't worry about it now, especially since he didn't have the luxury of time.

Loud cheers boomed from down the hall and he could hear the intro music taking up every inch of treble and bass available in the club.

He tapped out a quick message of his own: **Can't wait 2 C U**

No, that was cheesy and looked ridiculous, like something Donovan had written.

He tried again, making an effort to take his time and do this right: **Cannot wait to see you tonight. Don't stand me up. Promise?**

He added a winky face for good measure. One more for extra good measure and then carefully placed his phone in his locker and locked it for the first time in forever. He couldn't take any chances of his phone being stolen again and missing a message or replies being sent on his behalf. Damn Donovan. He'd check it every chance he got between numbers. Hopefully she wouldn't keep him waiting too long. The pandemonium, high-pitched and fully female, boomed louder.

"Time to go put some smiles on some faces. You ready?" asked Gabe.

"Always," said Jay. But something felt off, he didn't know what.

This girl ran like clockwork. Same walk, same route, same time every day. She didn't seem the type to run late. He knew it was ridiculous, but couldn't shake the feeling something wasn't right.

Damnit, this was not happening again. Hadn't he learned his lesson? He should have gone to pick her up and escorted her himself the second he'd discovered D's stupid stunt.

Jay thought about a girl he'd known when he first started at the club and what had happened to her on her way home one night. He'd danced for her as he had been doing regularly for the first three months of working there. They'd almost kissed until he realized she'd had one too many shots. That wasn't his style and he'd actually come to like talking to her. They'd agreed she was too drunk to drive herself home. Jay had asked her to stick around for the second show, figuring she was a regular of his and wouldn't have a problem with it. He'd give her a ride home but she'd insisted on getting back before curfew. Yeah, she'd also been just shy of eighteen which he found out that night. He'd pleaded with her to wait the two hours until he could drive her but when he came out to check on her between numbers, she'd disappeared.

The next day he'd found out what happened. She'd been date raped by some asshole they'd never caught. When it came time to file the report, she pieced together what she could and sadly, Jay's face was the last she remembered before she blacked out. His reputation for being flirty with the ladies hadn't helped his cause. Thankfully, he'd had the full support of Emma, the club, and his probation officer. The worst part was how badly he felt for what had happened to the girl. No charges were filed against him but he'd never let go of the knowledge that she'd come there that night to see him. And for that, she'd been so badly hurt.

What if something like that happened to Angel?

"Stop being paranoid," he whispered as he tested the black tie around his neck and then ran his fingers through his hair, habitually pushing it back from his face.

Wherever she is, she's fine. She'll be here.

Jay shook his head but fell in line with D, Gabe, Julian, Turtle, and Alec then took the stage. It was so loud. He could barely think. And it took all he had not to lunge himself at D. But then it wasn't really his friend's fault and he knew it. If he could have just been happy to watch her from the window. Jay rolled his shoulders and got into his stance. Maybe he was just crazy. Maybe when the curtain went up, she'd be there smiling that dazzling smile and like Mags had wanted, everything would turn out great. He still had no idea why but wanted to believe in that so badly.

Gabe counted them down, "One, two, three…" and then the dramatic, bass filled sound of strings took over as "Earned It" began to play. The ladies went wild with cheers as the music cued their six backs, wearing black suit pants and business shirts with undone ties. Jay couldn't help but smile to himself because he knew someone extraordinary and special was a Weeknd fan.

****

She couldn't stop her teeth from chattering.

So loud.

She was choking.

She screamed.

Pain exploded across her face. A palm shoved her lips up into her nose, shutting her up.

She had to get away. It hurt too much. Was she going to die?

"Am I going to die?" she asked, sobbing.

She didn't scream again. Just cried. She tried to think and not to think. She tried to breathe.

"Stop. Moving. You won't be told again."

The voice, one of three different voices, was cold and serious.

Her phone sounded. It was the fourth time. She heard it somewhere close in the background and she bit her tongue to keep silent. The phone's noise was one thing she could focus on rather than the intense, blistering pain hurting her so badly right now.

The other voices exchanged words that were hard to make out because they spoke low and on top of each other. The coldest one, the only one who had addressed her directly, suggested they shut up for a second and hand it to him.

Oh God. No.

That turned her into ashes.

She had to get her phone away from him. If he had it, he would have access to people she loved. People she had to protect. People whose names would show up in her most recent messages. Anyell. Her parents. Oh God. Jay.

Her vision was gone, her eyelids too swollen now, but still she kicked in his direction, trying. He grabbed at her ankle and shoved her back. For a second, the force of his heave sent her so far that it knocked her wrists free from the others who held her down. But they were too quick and scrambled to secure her again. Her bones cracked as evil squeezed her ankle and twisted. Popping and tearing left her in excruciating pain and she screamed until one of them covered her nose and mouth, silencing and nearly suffocating her. Inside, she pleaded.

Please.

Why?

No.

It was too late.

The cold voice leaked more poison and evil. She was forced into a sitting position from behind and her leg and back skin, no longer protected by the entirety of her dress, scraped against jagged spots on the asphalt. Evil's other hand jerked her chin. Her stomach ached and burned to throw up but she had to control what she could and sucked in air to keep it down. She felt what she believed was his spit splash across her face as he spoke. She trembled.

"Where are you? Jay wants to know. Are you okay? Jay asks. Yada yada yada. Seems like this Jay would really like to see you tonight. What do you say I tap out a little text? Invite him to our gathering. What should it say? Sorry babe. I'm just a couple blocks away." Evil paused and she cried softly with whatever she had left of tears and voice. It wasn't much. He continued. "I know. How about this: Jay, I could really use a ride. My feet are killing me." His grip hardened around her ankle and he slowly smashed it into the ground. "I'm just a few blocks away. Meet me at Vegas and Center Street and come alone baby. I wanna see you too—"

"No. Please. Don't." Guilt stabbed at her heart that for a moment, she'd wished for that very thing. For Jay to come save her from this. He was strong. He could make this all go away and punish these monsters for the terror they inflicted on her.

"Why not?" His voice became dark and completely void of anything she could render as human. "Why. Not?"

"Because." She had to think of something fast to keep Jay safe and away. "Because he means nothing to me."

"Well, you obviously mean something to him, you little liar. Give me a better reason."

Chills ran up her spine.

It would be easy to sob and retreat and beg. That would be heartless of her and she would not allow the beautiful sweet man she already cared so much for to suffer because of her weakness. "Please, I won't fight you anymore. But leave him out of it." She hated sharing anything personal with this monster but it might be what saved Jay. "He's at work. He can't leave. You'd be wasting your time."

All of a sudden, a bright flash of lights blinded her even behind her sealed lids. For one moment, she felt hope. Hope that those were headlights of a car passing by. Someone who would see a woman in the street at the mercy of human monsters. But the lights and the sound of the engine and tires faded and were replaced by dark laughter.

The next thing she felt was teeth. She almost screamed but there was no chance of that as the most hideous pain left her paralyzed.

In her mind, Kelley prayed and prayed and prayed. Not for herself, it was too late for that. She prayed God and the angels kept Jay safe. And away. Far away.

This was the end. She held tight to his smile, the sweet kiss he'd left on her cheek and prepared to leave this world. Holding her breath, she finally blacked out.

Chapter Seven

Is this heaven?
"She's my sister. Let me in. I just want to see her."

It was bright. Too bright. Rubbing alcohol and rubber obnoxiously hung around her face making breathing nauseating at best. Everything hurt yet everything was also numb.

Anyell. He was nearby and not happy.

Kelley lay there, staring.

For five seconds, she focused on the light switches. A few feet to the left and her eyes fixated on the waves the green curtain made. Slowly, including one long blink on the way over, her gaze eventually made it to the right, past the switches to the opening in the curtain. Red and black checkered slip-ons big enough to belong to her brother covered his big feet. No socks. He must have been in a hurry. Kelley held in a bucket of tears.

"Kell?" he called, his movement showing through the curtain's crack.

She should say she was right there, only a few feet away behind the curtain, but before she could get any of that out and aimed in his direction, a blinding pain took over in her stomach. Not inside, but on the skin. With hands that looked and felt completely foreign, stuck with needles and secured with tape, she made the mistake of patting along her abdomen. It was puffy and there was a barrier like she'd been wrapped in gauze. She patted again, lightly because the first time it had hurt so badly. It hurt again this time too. If she'd have been standing, she'd have doubled over and ended up on the floor. Her face became tight and twisted but she swallowed down the fire and practiced a slow breath.

"No," she whispered. "No."

Tears started to fall but when she saw her brother's hand reach inside the seam of the privacy curtain, she wiped them away, scraping her cheek with the medical tape laced around the back of her hand.

Like a giant rock, Anyell just stood there at first, clearly unsure of how to approach her. She must look as bereft and empty as she felt. If only she'd listened to him but no, she'd ignored her brother. Kelley tried to sit up to make it easier on him—the pain in his eyes was crushing—but when she did, her own pain was so unbearable that she screamed. Anyell ran immediately to her side.

"Kell?" he said, sounding tenderer than she'd ever heard him before. "What happened? Are you okay? They said you needed stitches. They said *hundreds* of stitches." He shook his head in disbelief. "When I came home this morning, you were gone." There was no room left on his beautiful caramel colored forehead for any more concern. Red streaks in the whites of his eyes made the crystal green even greener. She loved him so much and hated that she'd let this happen.

Saying I love you and I'm sorry would have been a good start but he kept on before she had the chance. "I found your note, Kell. God, do you know how fricking scared I was when the hospital called?"

She was so sorry. So very sorry she'd put him through this. It had been so hard having to give the nurse Anyell's contact information but she'd at least been lucid enough to know there was no way around it. As much as she'd preferred to have never had to let another soul in on what had happened, she'd have to eventually answer questions about the bandages and the limping she'd be doing around their house. The one thing Kelley refused to do was go into the sickening details. How could she when she still hadn't processed it for herself?

She was a fool and just wanted to be left alone.

Not touched.

Not seen.

A tear leaked from the corner of her eye when Anyell came closer.

He stood hunched over the side of her bed before ducking down and leaning over her to give her a hug as best he could. He kissed her forehead. She closed her eyes.

She loved him but could not do this. The air left the room and she silently prayed he would leave.

"What happened?"

Her eyes shot open. No, he had to stop asking her that. She could never answer that question. Never.

Worried wrinkles turned sharply into creases so severe she thought they'd become permanent parts of Anyell's face. God, she loved him. The thought wouldn't leave her alone. And every time it cycled through, it made her sadder for what she'd done and how she'd let him down. He looked so confused. Her brother had no concept that his sister had a mind and will of her own. What had happened? Tonight, that mind and will had been set. There was no one to blame but herself. She'd put herself in that place. No one else had done it. She closed her eyes and looked away, back to the familiar waves of the curtain.

Her stomach convulsed with more strangled tears. Pain searched out and found new places to rest within her.

Anyell. Until she healed and got past this somehow, she would have to pretend like she was fine. Like she'd just taken a nasty fall and ended up with severe cuts. That was what she'd tell her brother. The truth would kill something in him, the same way she felt dead inside right now.

But Jay.

She could never bring herself to look Jay in the face again. All the hopes she'd had for getting to know him, naïve as they were, had been stomped out by a viciousness she couldn't begin to comprehend. Three ugly, hideous and terrifying faces charged at the backs of her eyes and she had to seal them shut as tight as she could to blur the vision away. Kelley sucked in a breath, trying to keep it together for her brother, forming a story they both could live with. Because the truth was inconceivable.

"What friend did you go visit? Where is your car? This is her fault, this friend of yours," said Anyell.

He assumed so wrongly. Kelley just lay there, knowing she had to say something soon.

He skimmed his hand along her bruised and cut cheekbone, reminding her he was more sorry than pissed right now, even though it was hard to differentiate with his tone being so raw. He squeezed her hand and stared at her for long minutes. Any minute, the helplessness building up on Anyell's face would have nowhere else to go. She couldn't just ignore him. That would be selfish and cruel.

"I don't know what exactly happened. I hit my head in the fall and blacked out."

It wasn't a lie. That had been part of the nightmare. She had no idea how something like this could have happened. How human beings could do what had been done to her.

"The first time I leave you alone and this happens. I can never leave you alone again and you seriously need to consider this friend. I don't get it. Did she help you at all? Geez Kell, you look like you were hit by a car and dragged down the street."

She just shook her head, deciding it was easier to let Anyell keep his assumptions. None of this was Jay's fault and there was no way on earth she'd utter his name in front of her brother, or anyone for that matter. Anyell would go crazy and lay blame where it did not belong. Jay hadn't laid a hand on her. They'd shared one innocent walk, an even sweeter peck on the cheek and a couple looks that said there might be more coming, but that was it. The night had gone nothing like she'd planned.

Pain medication had her groggy but she remembered she wanted to ask the nurse about her personal belongings. Her phone. She prayed it had made its way to the hospital because it was how she planned to cut all ties with Jay, fledgling as they were.

"Not my friend's fault," she said through a morphine induced yawn.

"You're right. It's my fault. I never should have left you alone," said Anyell, stuck on that train of thought. "Cliff could have done this without me."

"No," she forced herself to say. "You are learning the business so you can take over someday." God, it hurt to talk and her tongue felt triple its size. "It's your dream, Anyell. What you work so hard for."

Anyell leaned down and whispered into her ear, "Not at the price of my family." He paused like he wasn't sure how to continue. His green eyes swam around until they settled on her again. She tried to focus. He looked down and then up one last time. "You fell? Because some of these cuts and bruises on your face look like more than a fall." His voice became even softer and she could only hear his brotherly love coming through. He whispered even more so, presumably so that no one else in the vicinity would hear. "If this is something other than a fall, you can tell me. If," he paused and the worry drew his brows together with a pinch, "if this was done to you, you can tell me that too." He pulled back a few inches, wiped a few pieces of bang from her eyes and searched her face.

She could only shake her head no.

If she knew the monsters who'd done this, it would have been so much worse. As it was, her attackers remained nameless strangers and that was how she wanted them to stay. Having their repulsive faces lurk behind her every thought was torment enough.

"This was an accident, Yell. This wasn't your fault. I know you have questions, but I don't remember much. I just want to go home, recuperate, and get back to school."

For the first time in her life, she saw her brother's eyes really tear up as they sat there alone. He swallowed tightly. His jaw buckled and she saw fury break across his face for a split second before he bowed his head, probably trying to hide it from her. "Do I need to call the police? Whoever did this, whatever this is, is out there."

He was too perceptive for his own good. Others might have dismissed Anyell's intellect but she never would.

Whatever this was.

What an accurate description.

She shook her head no, that he didn't need to make that call.

If her brother had asked if she'd been raped, it probably would have been easier for him to understand than what the monsters had viciously done to her. They were out there and could hurt someone else. What she couldn't tell Anyell was that she'd already spoken to the police and filed a report. Her memory of those first moments of being brought in to the ER was a blur but at least there was some record of what had happened, even if the details she'd been able to give were sketchy. Her hands began to shake.

"You're shaking, Kell."

"Just cold," she said with a shudder.

She pivoted to the right and the pain woke with a new ferocity. She had to remember to stay still. Each time the wounds on her stomach rubbed against the bandages, it was like fire and ice erupting in her skin all over again. She shook her head no, again, but knew if she didn't give him something else, his protective heart would fight on her behalf. Kelley could not have her brother digging into this any further. "I told them what I could," she said in a small voice. "Please don't ask me anymore questions. I just want to get out of here as soon as possible and go home and go to sleep."

Her brother nodded and kissed her hand although his eyes and face said he was far from being able to just forget it all. He then left their curtained off area and Kelley could hear him speaking with the nurse about her discharge.

The nurse began to go into how to clean her wounds and that was the motivation Kelley needed to make her voice loud. "Anyell," she called out. It worked. He was back by her side and the nurse with him.

"What? Are you in pain?"

Yes she was but that wasn't what she'd hollered about. There was no way she could let her brother see what had been done to her. "Please excuse us, Yell. I need to speak to my nurse alone. Please."

He hesitated but then stepped out.

"Please don't tell him," she whispered to the nurse who seemed to understand. "I will be able to change my own bandages."

Kelley's eyelids started to feel even heavier.

"Of course. And I'll discharge you at the end of my shift. That gives you five more hours to rest." The nurse patted her forehead and smoothed Kelley's bangs out of her face. "If you'd like, I can ask your brother to wait in the waiting room."

"Thank you," was all she was able to say until she remembered the other thing she needed to ask about. "Was my phone brought in with my things?"

At first, the nurse's mouth scrunched up like she doubted it but then after looking in a few containers below Kelley's bed, she came back up with a soft smile. "Here you go, dear. I'll be sure and have your brother wait outside. You look like you need some privacy. And sweetheart, remember that we swabbed your wounds when you came in. We always make our best effort to honor confidentiality but you should be aware that you may be contacted in regards to those findings and your report."

She nodded. The nurse understood her need for privacy and Kelley mustered what was probably a very sad looking attempt at a grateful smile. Once she was alone again, she went to find Jay's name in her contact list and compose her goodbye message when she saw that she had an unread message from him. Actually, she had six unread messages from Jay. More pain. More shoving it aside. She pressed the button to read through each one, needing to see his words as much as she knew she had to forget all about them.

Her gut twisted at the first one because it was him being flirty and kind and asking her not to stand him up. The second one made her chin quiver. The message had clearly been interrupted because it left off mid-sentence with the last words being, "You're in the audience right? I know you're probably just hiding, being shy. I'll keep looking for—"

Messages three and four and five reminded her of her brother. Time checks, questions of whether she was okay or not. Apologies for not driving her himself.

Number six. Number six made her cry. It opened to a selfie of his face, with one eyebrow hiked up as if he was saying, "You're standing me up, aren't you?" but like he didn't mean it because he was also grinning. It was accompanied by so many of his perfect words that her tears turned into a steady stream of heartbreak marching down her cheek: **I'm not sure where you are, sweetheart. But I promise not to take it personal. I know I came on strong this morning and probably scared you. I'm sorry for that. I'll do better next time. I hope there's a next time. I also hope you're okay. I can tell you're capable and all, but do me a favor. Call me. Just wanna know I didn't drag you out here and now you're somewhere hurt. Call. Me. P.S. I'd really like to see you again but I understand if you need to take your time. I am a very patient guy. See ya, angel.** And three winky faces she could barely make out through her tears.

Before replying, she put the phone screen to sleep and held it to her battered and scraped chest. Tiny slices of pain bit back at the intrusion against her tender skin but she held it there, thinking of what to say. If she went the route of the truth, it would kill him. She could tell he'd take the blame. All of it, and probably never be able to forgive himself. How could he even look at her if he knew? Even if she only did half the truth like she'd done with her brother, if things grew between them, he'd eventually want to see her. She may have never experienced intimacy first hand but hadn't been born yesterday. She hadn't even seen herself yet but the memories brought on the urge to throw up.

Kelley wiped at her forehead, sniffling, her body racked with serious physical pain. What other option did she have but to say something that cut things off?

Finally, she opened the message back up but first scrolled to the picture he'd sent, yearning for him in ways she couldn't understand. She gazed at it, wishing things had turned out differently. Oh the smiles they could have had. She kissed his image and then wrote a message that would ensure he never try to contact her again: **Jay, you seem great. I'm fine, just not interested. Didn't want you to worry.**

Instant tears pricked her eyes at the lies.

But reading over it again, she realized she'd been too kind at the end. She backspaced until the message ended at "not interested." Heaving, she pressed send and then let the phone fall to her side, becoming buried somewhere in the hospital sheets.

Her heart nearly exploded.

The nurse was by her side as soon as she cried out with the loud sob. As if understanding everything, Nurse Analisa just rested her chin on top of Kelley's head and held her gently. "It will be okay, dear."

No, it wouldn't, she thought as fresh sobs racked her upper body, causing new and immense amounts of pain to her wounds. Her words were cruel and the last things she ever wanted to say to him. Sweet, kind, adorable Jay. The guy she'd known all of twenty-four hours and yet knew somewhere deep inside he'd been so special. Their paths had been meant to cross yesterday morning. There would be no telling of that extraordinary first meeting of theirs now or ever. She could never let anyone see what had been done to her. Especially not him. Not ever. And she would never, never in a million years, allow his name to be tied to this ugly attack.

****

"You need me to spot you?"

Jay ignored D and got up from the workout bench he'd been sitting on then left through the gym's back door. Thoroughly confused and in disbelief, he fell back against it and let out a mouthful of hot air.

"Something's not right," he muttered to himself. The message was brief and cold, two things she couldn't be even if she tried. He'd just scared her with coming on too strong. He'd give her time. She'd realize he was just a shit for brains goofball whose biggest crime was wanting to get to know her better. Jay looked off to the side, trying to think of what he should do. In the end, he couldn't help but reply back: **No worries. Take your time.**

He put his phone away and returned to the gym, hitting it extra hard and vowing to be patient. He needed to sweat because hell if she hadn't just split his heart in two.

Chapter Eight

Twelve long months and a couple weeks later,
July...

"I wish I could bring you with me, cat," she said and set the still unnamed gray puffy mess on the bookshelf closest to her front door. Kelley fished her keys out of her pocket then slid her fingers into the rings and squeezed. Anyell's "super early impromptu Christmas present" sat there looking up at her. She tried hard to envision stabbing a would-be attacker in the eyes, but somehow, that look of need being aimed at her gained priority. Kelley had been reluctant to keep the kitty and it had only been one week, but she was already wrapped around the little mess's paws. "I'll be right back," she said and scratched its head. "Just gonna go grab your paperwork from Dr. Cool."

It would be a short trip. They always were nowadays.

Taking a deep breath and closing her eyes, she waited a moment until it passed. When Kelley opened her eyes, she saw the fur ball had already gone to cat nap heaven. God how she wished it were that easy and rubbed her own tired eyes.

She stared at the doorknob, ashamed at how ugly it was compared to the rest of the beautiful door. It didn't used to be that way. She cringed for having altered the elegant block of wood but the additional deadbolt helped calm her nerves. Mesmerized by the dull silver, she lost track of time in the odd moment. Her eyes jumped from the bottom knob up to the additional deadbolt just above it and she silently thanked her brother for installing it. Moving her head to the right, Kelley checked the crack between the door and its frame where she could see the bolt was securely lodged into its crevice. She wrapped her hand around the knob and tested it. Kelley rubbed her lips together, trying to focus, and stepped back.

"You will leave this house right now. Someone is depending on you," she scolded herself and glanced at the napping cat whose legs straightened for a moment and toes splayed wide before curling back up. "I could learn a thing or two from you, couldn't I?" The fur on its head was so soft as she scratched the gray noggin.

Not only did her new friend need its official paperwork but also its eye drops. The poor thing had faulty tear glands and without the drops, she'd been told its eyes would become cloudy and irritated.

Adoring it with a few more head scratches, she said, "We won't let that happen. I promise." She was so uncomfortable leaving the house but for this sweet creature, she'd do it.

Anyell hollered at her from the driveway and she barely heard him due to everything in the house being closed. Her brother was forcing her to drive her car today with the promise he'd be right behind in his truck. Ashamed and humiliated at her inadequacies, Kelley wanted to drive without being so needy. But then again, a part of her wanted lots of things she knew weren't feasible. Like the end of nightmares. One of these days, she'd open that front door and feel the sun melt through her skin and into her bones again the way it had *that* morning.

Sweat moistened her palms and she wiped them dry against her pants as she pushed *those* thoughts away.

Through the glass cut-out of the door and the painfully bright sunrays, she saw Anyell coming up the walkway. After a fast three count and with practiced precision, she clicked the top dead bolt to the left, then the center one to the left as well, and then dropped to the doorknob lock and twisted it to the right. Finally, she tugged the door open, counting the clicks and steps as she went.

Anyell looked at her with nothing but calm on his face and then held his hand out which she took right away. They walked hand in hand until reaching her car. That was when he let go and made some distance between them. With her brother standing a couple feet away, Kelley knew it was all up to her.

"You got this, Kell," he said.

"What if it doesn't start?" she asked him, eyeballing her seat through the driver side window.

"It will. I just checked it this morning. You'll see as soon as you sit down and drive her for the first time."

She shouldn't have any hang ups with this car. It was new, new to her at least, and yes, she knew her brother had worked hard to bolster their savings and get her one of the safest models out there.

"But it's sat here for months. That's not good for cars."

"Like I said, Kell, I start her up every morning. I'll be following right behind you. I promise."

A tear leaked down her cheek. "I'm sorry." She hoped it said everything she felt about being ashamed for her weaknesses and the ways in which she had yet to heal and move on. The dark places she was still stuck and the way she just wanted to hide. The daily reminders she whispered to walk herself through mundane tasks that most did without thought. Anyell heard and saw it all. "I'm sorry," she said again and then silently repeated the Japanese proverb she'd read and never forgotten for a paper she'd written on the country's horrific 2011 natural disaster.

Fall down seven times, get up eight.

In her peripheral, she saw his knees start to move but then it was as if he changed his mind and stood planted. "I'll give you a hug once we get there. Now let's go. Get in." His voice held no wiggle room.

He'd make a great father someday. She could trust him. Knowing she'd never do this if she couldn't stop staring at the handle, she squeezed her clicker and as soon as the locks popped open, she pulled on the door and got in. There was no time for pausing or else she'd just chicken out so she kept up the flow of her fast momentum and stuck the key in the ignition, deciding now wasn't the time for settling into that "new car" feel for the seats, knobs and dials. She turned the key and the engine came to life immediately. Anyell ran around to hop into his truck and then he backed out so she could also back out and end up in front of him on their street.

"You've got this," she said as she rolled in reverse and then crept forward.

The pet sanctuary where Dr. Cool worked was just on the outskirts of Boulder City. Five blocks into the drive, she saw people out walking her old route. At the stop sign, she looked around, foolishly hoping for the impossible.

As if on cue, or maybe he just appeared because she was looking for someone who fit the bill, a young man in a track suit jogged by with ear phones in his ears. He even had a head full of blond hair. After all this time, she still remembered that day like it had been yesterday. Jay. She studied this young man as he passed her and she continued to slowly keep pace with him until he turned left and went on his way and she kept driving straight, followed by her brother.

He wasn't Jay.

She guessed there probably wasn't another like that man on God's green earth. The wish of having the chance to apologize to Jay had gone unfulfilled for so long now and again like always, she reminded herself why that wouldn't serve anyone's interests but her own. There were days when she wished she hadn't changed her phone number, effectively cutting off their communications, but knew it was for the best. She'd fallen so hard for him in those thirty minutes of their one and only meeting and knew reading a text or hearing his voice would dominate and conquer every reason she had for keeping her distance. Staying inside was the only choice. She'd made it and abided by it.

One whole year, she thought to herself and exited the freeway to pull into the pet sanctuary's parking lot. For a Sunday, it seemed awfully busy. Her scalp itched all of a sudden.

"There are so many cars," she whispered to herself, still not having undone her seatbelt. She put her car in park and her brother, who normally would come to open her door, stood back and waited. Kelley pulled down on her long sleeves, making sure they came well below her wrists and adjusted the collar until she no longer felt warm summer air on her neck. "It's time. You can't keep waiting. Can't keep locked inside the house."

The hands-on portions of her studies were the only ones remaining now that she'd completed every possible online credit she could. And, she'd do good to name her new cat, which reminded her it was time to get her butt out of the car and go fetch the eye drops. She climbed out of the car. Anyell, dressed in a much more appropriate sleeveless shirt and shorts, flanked her. They walked to the sanctuary entrance together and something about the sun, this time, looked nice shining up in the sky, even though it was blazing hot out. It was such a nice reprieve from the darkness she'd fallen into. But she knew the real question was whether she could do this without her brother.

This being the little things in life.

You have to. You can't stay hidden your whole life. What would be the point in that? Still, the depravity of that night just wouldn't go away. *Focus on how strong you are. How strong you had to be to have survived. Today, you are brand new, mi'hija.*

The words of Nurse Analisa, the one who had cared for her on such a compassionate and understanding level, ran through her mind every day and again now as she hesitated at the door.

"After you," said Anyell and ushered her inside.

Kelley stepped inside and had a quick look around while Anyell gave her a nod and a supportive glance and then went off on his own, probably in search of a good guard dog for his and Cliff's supply yard. At least that would be his excuse for slipping away. She knew he was right in doing it.

Apparently it was an adoption event day and signs decorated the walls, the explanation for the full parking lot. Pets, presumably waiting to be adopted, laid about everywhere. Especially the cats. The smell still managed to be pleasant, with more pet grooming product in the air than anything else. Off to her right was an area where a larger crowd stood huddled. Something about the group drew her eye. In between the waving of handheld fans and bobbing heads trying to get a better look, a few heads stood taller than the rest and appeared to have much more bared shoulders and arms, only wearing tank tops. Kelley nearly rubbed her own completely covered arms, but quickly became fixated on one.

She couldn't tear her eyes away.

The man's shoulder length blond hair moved every which way because a small brown puppy with more energy than a lightning storm kept poking its head through the curtain of strands and licking everything within tongue's reach. Just then the puppy lurched forward, nearly springing from the man's shoulders but in a fast twist, he spun around and miraculously saved the puppy from what would have been a long, unpleasant fall to the ground.

Kelley's jaw dropped.

There was nothing for her to do but stare, a rarity anymore, especially around men, and she willed her glance to fall to the floor.

Except it didn't. Couldn't. Wouldn't.

With their eyes locked on each other, Kelley forgot to breathe.

The puppy dove again, this time toward her. Distance shrank. A blur of bare, solid shoulders trespassed into her space as brown fur sailed through the air and Kelley sprinted on instinct toward it. The next thing she knew, her entire face was coated in dog saliva.

"I think she likes you," he said, his voice as peaceful as she remembered. But did he remember her?

Kelley's heart added and subtracted beats at random. He reached a long, strong arm out and petted the puppy's head to calm it as Kelley held it like a lifejacket to her chest.

"It's okay little one, she had that effect on me too. Hey you, long time no see." He winked at her but in his eyes, she could see the way in which he held back.

What did she say to the man she both feared and longed seeing the most in this world? Nothing. She said nothing. Just closed her eyes and held the puppy tight.

Chapter Nine

The smart thing to do would be to play it cool and act unaffected. Jay had been accused of many things in his life but holding back had never been one of them. Damn, was he really this easy? She'd blown him off for a year and yet here he stood, unable to turn around and walk away. Yeah, he was damaged people, especially when it came to *her* and those serious eyes. He watched as the puppy he'd been posing with for today's charity work photos licked her entire face up and down. Crap, he couldn't help but smile, a real one, because even though it hurt that she'd stood him up, at least he finally knew she was okay. Alive and breathing. Someone with a heavy hand landed it on his shoulder.

"Yo."

Donovan. Great. Keep your mouth shut, bro. The last thing Jay needed was to be busted out about his ridiculous amount of time pining over this girl. D didn't say anything but instead reached out and extricated the little Min-pin from her face and arms and handed the energy ball off to Jay.

D stuck out his hand.

"Hey," D said with that suave smile Jay knew all too well. "That little puppy looks great on you. Adoption fees are waived today, you know. We're just taking donations if you're feeling charitable. And photos. Lots of photos."

No D did not just wag his eyebrows at her. WTF?

Jay stood there speechless. He couldn't see anything but her head with the uncomfortable looking green turtleneck sweater pulled up to just below her jaw, but the blush was evident on her cheeks and he imagined it had started down below her collar bone. A memory of watching it spread from there all the way up her neck to the tips of her cute ears the day he'd joined her and stolen her earbud washed over him, erasing some of the anger he'd felt at her complete denial of him since that day.

Damn if he hadn't gone through every scenario he possibly could to explain why she'd just completely written him off. Was she too ashamed when she'd found out he took his clothes off for a living? The more her cheeks reddened and her discomfort grew at D's flirty smiles, the more Jay thought that must be it. And what look had she given Jay just now? She'd been stiff and rigid and tight looking.

But what did he say to the girl who'd broken his heart? His fricking foolish heart. He'd never, never fallen for a girl that fast. Ever. Jay had vowed he never would again. Everything returned to being just for fun, like it always had been with him.

Before *her.*

The most ridiculous part? All that pining and worrying after a girl whose real name he didn't even know. D gave him a sideways glance as if to say, "I got this, you can make your exit now, foolio." Yeah, he probably should. But then she blinked a few fast times and Jay knew she was about to speak. Hell if he wasn't stuck in this same spot, waiting to hear her voice again after all this time.

"Oh, I don't know. A puppy is a big responsibility." Strange. She said the words and they were the same ones he heard all the time at these events when he and the guys were trying their best to get the ladies to adopt the rescues. But she said it like the thought actually scared her. "It's very cute. But I just don't think I can." She started to back away and Jay couldn't ignore the way she used one hand to pull up on the neck of her sweater and the other to tug the long sleeve downward. She then crossed her arms over her stomach in a low hug.

Coupled with that was the sound in her voice again. That note of sadness. He doubted she was just blowing them off like many of the ladies who just wanted their pictures with the hot guys but had no intentions of adopting. The more they all three just stood there, the more intense her face became, the tighter her fists balled up, that was until the puppy got itself free from D's clutches and leaped for *her* again.

Jay couldn't just not say anything. "I don't know," he said and then glanced down at his own feet and then hers for a second then looked back up. "Looks like a perfect fit to me, Miss. I'm sorry, I never caught your name."

Why the hell was he doing this to himself? Yeah, clearly D thought the same thing with that WTF look on his face.

Standing there holding her lips together tightly, she looked around as if she was searching for someone, then at the puppy and then at him. Sort of at him. She didn't seem able to lock stares with him again since she'd first seen him just now.

"Oh, um, my name..."

"Kelley," came a deep voice from behind Jay but Jay just kept his eyes trained on her.

Kelley. He thought it over a few times. Finally, he knew.

"Kelley," Jay said quietly.

"Everything okay?" said the voice again before its owner came into Jay's view.

Ah hell. ESPN went and stood right next to her. Well that explained the past year and why she'd never showed up.

The guy's eyes scanned Jay and D and yeah, all that crap dudes said to each other without really saying it passed between them. She looked back and forth from Jay to ESPN. Jay hadn't seen the jock in as long as he hadn't seen *her*. It was as if they'd vanished off the planet.

D spoke up first. "Hey man, thanks for coming out today." With that man-on-man vibe the guys reserved for interacting with other dudes, he offered up a fist bump. "You here to adopt?" He said it nice and calm, even under the guy's wary stares. This dude was fit, just like Jay and D, and Jay knew he wasn't intimidated in the least but it was then that he recognized that look. It wasn't impossible. Families came in all shapes and sizes. Jay could swear that look was 100% big brother. And then he looked at his and D's muscle shirts with the large "Mantasy" logo spread across their chests.

ESPN looked at her, at *Kelley,* and softened immediately.

"I was telling your girlfriend that there are no adoption fees today, just donations," D said, probably thinking he was smooth. Jay just shook his head.

"Sister," she said, confirming Jay's assumption.

Jay would like way more control over the situation and the players at this point. Meaning he'd really like a moment alone with her. To talk and find out what had happened. There was way more going on that he was sensing from her and the brother. His protectiveness was extra strength and her energy kept switching. Hot to cold, hot to cold. Maybe the puppy was a good idea for them. It seemed like they needed a tension buster and that little thing scrambling to stay in her arms every time she tried to hand it off to D would do the trick.

"Okay guys, well I think someone is convinced she already has a new mommy," said D pointing at the pup.

"She's pretty cute, Kell," said the brother, standing with his arms folded over his chest, unnecessarily pushing his biceps beyond their normal size. "I guess we could bring the cat back and exchange it for this one."

"No!" she said, clearly surprising the three of them and herself. Her pretty eyes popped and their eyebrows all shot up at her shout. "I mean, no. That would be cruel to give back the cat. You said it already had at least three homes this year."

"That is a sad fact for a lot of these pets," D chimed in.

ESPN and Kelley both looked at D and then at each other.

"Well I just thought since you haven't named it yet. Maybe I should have let you come pick out your own pet is all. I doubt the cat will care and I'm sure these dudes won't have any problems getting someone to take it home." Jay's heart had no business soaring when he watched her eye down her brother after that comment, but it did. "No offense," the brother said to him and D.

"None taken. Hey, I have to get back to the rest of the rescues. My man Jay can stay here and help you all decide on this pretty girl." D left with a wave to go back to the main adoption area. Jay wished again for one less brother and struggled with how speechless he still was. He had to say something though.

He guessed it would be doggie facts.

"So this one. She's small but I'll let you in on a little secret. She's actually not a puppy anymore. This is her fifth adoption event that I've been at. She's come close a couple times but all that energy, I think it scares people off." His gaze dropped and a sting zapped him right in the heart at knowing that sounded a lot like him. "She's such a sweetheart though." And then he took a huge and probably really stupid chance but around this girl, it was like he was back in the seventh grade and just discovering his moves and winning lines. "She needs someone just as sweet to look out for her."

Kelley's mouth formed an immediate "Oh". Her brother frowned simultaneously.

"Do you know my sister?" he asked without mincing his words.

Jay just looked at Kelley with as little pressure as he could manage and tried to tell her with his eyes that this was up to her. He remembered how sure he was that she'd been too uncomfortable to come and see him dance. He wouldn't force her to own up to any knowledge of him now if she didn't want to. It hurt like hell, but that wasn't his style.

Over the noise of the barking puppies and adoring Club Mantasy fans who'd come out today, she finally spoke up. "Jay is an old friend."

"That's it?" ESPN asked.

"That's it," she said and stared right into Jay's eyes as she held the dog who was now resting calmly in her arms.

What more did she need to say?

Shocked didn't begin to describe what he felt inside.

She'd publicly claimed him. In front of her brother who clearly didn't like the thought of his sister associating with a guy who was wearing the tagline that he was every girls' man fantasy. But that one small gesture of hers and the sadness in her eyes let him know there had to be more to the story of why she'd gone radio silent for so long. Jay just had to decide if he was willing to risk it happening again to find out why. Well, he'd been accused of many things throughout his life, as the saying went.

"My volunteer shift actually ended just before we ran into each other. What do you say we start the paper work to make you this one's new home and then go grab a bite to eat? I'm starving. Have lunch with me, Kelley."

He expected a single shot of hell no was about to come tunneling out of her brother. Funny enough, he didn't really care and he wasn't backing down.

****

It was all too much. The new cat. The even newer dog because she knew she couldn't leave there without the sweet thing. Anyell and his body heat hugging her closer and closer the tighter he squeezed in on her personal space.

Him.

God, him. As heart wrenching as it had been having to deny him when he was nowhere in her physical vicinity compared not even a smidgen to what it felt like now each time she tried to get the words out that she was sorry but couldn't. Those words would not fall out of her mouth no matter how hard she tried to force them. Kelley had to get control of her thoughts. This had to be all logic and no emotion.

Remember why you can't, Kelley. Remember.

At that, she did remember. The deadening of her heart always came back first. That hollow feeling of defeat, knowing she'd been caught by evil people and would not be escaping them no matter how hard she fought to get free. The fear she'd felt that night came over her now like it always did, as ice cold pokers stabbed at the base of her skull. She had to blink because she was so afraid of going blind and everyone seeing it happen. She gritted her teeth.

*No, no, no, no. Not here. Not in front of all these
people.*

Him.

But no matter how hard she tried to regain control
of the panic, her fingertips went numb until her hands
became useless and she handed the puppy off to Anyell.
She squeezed herself, tucking her arms into themselves
across her body. She had no explanation for why the
physical pain of what had been done to her never seemed
to come. Maybe because once you felt something that
horrendous, you knew no amount of physical pain would
ever match it again. It was like her body was saying, why
bother?

Anyell fumbled around with the dog as Kelley
stepped back, having to trust it was in good hands. She
must get out of there now.

No one said anything directly to the other but she
could hear a mix of male voices trying to reach her as she
made a break for the exit. With her two desensitized
hands, she pushed the door with all her might and met the
sweltering heat and blinding daylight as soon as she was
on the outside.

Breathe, she thought as she fell against the
building. Just as her sight adjusted to the bright sun and
she was about to make her way to her car, she froze. This
truly terrified her, but she couldn't remember what color
it was. Nothing came to mind. She began to shake and a
severe wave of embarrassment and confusion washed
over her as she searched the lot, still blanking. There
were so many cars and not one of them stood out.

All she could see was her old green Pontiac.

All she could remember was how it had died on
her that night.

And then teeth.

Kelley's breathing became too shallow.

She squeezed her eyes shut.

Chapter Ten

"Aren't you going to go after her?" Jay asked, wishing he knew the guy's name. He was Kelley's brother and it would be nice to have a civilized conversation right now.

ESPN kept his post at the glass door where he could obviously still see Kelley. Jay wanted to trust him but his instincts shouted to go after her. But it had been what, a twenty minute reunion, if you could call it that, after a year of nothing? The guy clearly had no idea who Jay was. That's right, because he'd met Kelley one time. For thirty minutes. D was right. Jay's heart was screwed for life. Which meant he and her brother needed to have a conversation. A quick one, but words needed to be exchanged all the same, before Jay ran out there after her.

"Jay, by the way." Jay said it firmly as he stuck his hand out toward the less-than-thrilled guy. His greeting was silence and ego at first but then it was like ESPN had no choice. Two guys and a puppy, all hinged on helping the girl who'd just run hysterically out the door, managed to work in Jay's favor and got them talking rather than brawling.

"Anyell. How do you know my sister?"

Okay, at least it was a start.

"We used to walk the same route. A long time ago," he added. That got him a glare but Jay felt his question was way more pressing. "Again, why aren't you going out there? She's clearly freaked out and I'm not trying to be a jerk here, but if you don't go, I will."

They looked at each other and Jay could tell Kelley's brother hadn't appreciated his tone. "She's never mentioned you and if you knew her from walking, you'd have known me too. And uh, no, whoever you are, you're not going out there after my sister." A look was exchanged like Jay must be delusional to have even suggested it.

That's right because she'd only been by herself the one time with him. A horrible feeling hit him in the gut just then when he thought about that. The way her brother said "knew" in the past tense added to his questions about where she'd been this whole time. What had happened after that day? Why had he never seen her and her brother walking past his apartment again? He figured they'd moved but here they were at the pet sanctuary not so far from their neighborhood.

"We ran into each other once and she helped me." He quit right there, not liking the intensity growing in Anyell's eyes.

"What did she help you with?"

Damn, answering that was asking for it. Jay remembered how cute she'd been when he tugged her earbud out. He wondered if big bro had a clue as to her scandalous playlist. Trying to think quickly, he spit out, "Directions." It wasn't a complete lie. Meeting her that day had definitely sent him on a wild goose chase of sorts and ultimately had left him feeling nothing but lost. All the nights he'd spent texting her, genuinely worried, with no reply and all the miles he'd put in on foot and in his car scouring the neighborhood and coming up empty. Funny how easy he'd let that go just now with her. But the short answer seemed to float. "Look, I'm just a friend and I just want to help and it looks like she needs some help. So…" Jay fake saluted Kelley's brother and pushed the door open.

"You're not going out there, man. Not happening. I don't know you. Nobody gets near Kelley," said Anyell as the door came slamming back shut.

Jay could tell he meant every word of it. What he didn't understand was the fire behind it all and how the guy looked about ready to kill with his bare hands. Jay was just trying to help. Man, that day she'd been out on her own must have been like being freed from the gates of a maximum security prison if this was the norm. He reminded himself not to smart off though.

"I genuinely just want to make sure she's okay."

"Why?" The words came from Anyell, filled with accusation only the way a brother could dish it out. He'd used that tone a few times where Mags had been concerned.

Jay rubbed his forehead, out of brilliant ideas and avoidance tactics. Maybe if any of his sister's boyfriends had ever been even a shred of truthful with him, he wouldn't have hated them all so much. Maybe the hate he'd had for them all wouldn't have clouded his judgment the one time a good guy did turn up in the bunch. Jay hated that he'd pushed one of the good ones away and ultimately how his sister had ended up dying without ever having been loved the right way. He decided there was only one way to handle this. "Honestly? I don't know. I mean you're right, I don't really know your sister all that well. I met her one time. We walked her route. She seemed like a nice person. I asked her out. And then I never heard from her again. That's the truth. That was a year ago. Haven't seen her until today."

"A year ago?"

"Yeah."

"And this business with you asking her out. Where did you go?"

"Like I said, nowhere. She never showed up. Never answered my calls either. I never even knew her name until today."

Anyell's posture deflated back down to just ripped and not ripped on steroids. Jay sensed he'd come across as genuine to him. Even though he still didn't look thrilled. While Jay knew it had been important to get this out in the open if he wanted any chance of talking with Kelley, the convo had gone on long enough and he really had nothing left to say.

Anyell rubbed at the scruff of his thin goatee, which reminded Jay a lot of his buddy Turtle, and shook his head back and forth like his thoughts were giving him a serious headache. "You say she never showed up. Where was she supposed to meet you?"

Damn. He did not want to go there right now and what was up with this inquisition? Things had gone relatively well. The second he said he'd invited Kelley to the club where he worked, Anyell would revolt on him. He knew it. He thought for a moment. *Be as honest as you can.* "I asked her to meet me where I work so we could go grab something to eat after my shift finished." The more ESPN questioned and eyeballed him, the more Jay worried about what had happened to Kelley that night.

"Where do you work?"

Amazed that Anyell hadn't put two and two together yet what with the Club Mantasy tank top and all, Jay kept his fingers crossed that the realization wouldn't come in the next couple minutes. The club was off of one of Boulder City's busiest streets, lined with several businesses, any of which could be his place of employment. "Nevada Boulevard."

Just say it. But he couldn't. Not yet. Something told him it would kill any chance he had of breaking through big bro's barrier to speak with her. He was beginning to realize what a miracle it had been to catch her that day on her own. Kelley's brother clearly wasn't ready to hear about his chosen profession even though it was the reason he was here helping pets find homes today. Most people missed that noble aspect.

The two of them seemed to be having yet another silent conversation with their eyes so Jay took the liberty to glance outside to make sure Kelley was still there. She was. Still going up and down the aisles and stopping at random cars.

When he gave his attention back to Anyell, Jay was sure he heard the words "private business" murmured. Yeah, he'd like some privacy back too. Jay hadn't felt this exposed in a very long time and that said a lot coming from a guy who took his clothes off for a living.

Jay stood there waiting, as Anyell remained stoic and covered his mouth with his hand, rubbing at his goatee.

Enough already!

Not like any of that posturing mattered much because the sight of Kelley outside in this worrisome state had Jay about ready to crawl out of his skin. That day walking she'd been young, sure, and adorable in a naïve sort of way, but he'd seen strength in her eyes, her body, and the energy she gave off. She'd been excited about life, starved for it, and when he'd first come up on her, she'd been ready to protect herself. There'd been no missing the way she clutched her phone and made a tight fist around it. That girl out there right now, the one he'd bumped into while wrangling the puppy, that girl was off. He just didn't know why.

Enough talking already.

That voice inside his head started leveling threats that if he didn't get his ass out there to her, he was going to haunt Jay for the rest of his miserable life.

He didn't know why he said it exactly the way he did, but his next words came from his heart. "I'm not the bad guy here. I'd never hurt her. She clearly needs someone. Now."

They looked together one last time as Jay went for the door again.

"Wait. Give her five minutes out there on her own," said Anyell, stopping Jay with his muscled arm. The guy was even stronger than he looked. Well, at least she had an able bodied protector. Wherever she'd gone. Whatever she was hiding from. He got up into Jay's face to say the rest, leaving only a couple inches between them. "You think it's easy watching my big sister out there suffering like that? It's not. But you don't know anything about her situation. So this is where you get to trust me, got it? Not the other way around. She needs to handle this. On her own." Anyell served each word to him with purpose and finality.

Big sister? Jay would have thought it was the other way around but then he knew a thing or two about little brothers and the things they'd do for their big sisters.

Jay didn't pretend to understand the strange request but by the look on ESPN's face, the guy genuinely believed this was necessary. Making a scene with him wouldn't benefit anyone.

Fine. He'd wait five minutes.

But he'd be doing it from the glass door where he could see her. It was hard to make out, but he was sure she was the one who had just walked up to and stopped at Gabe's car. She rested there with her hand on the trunk.

Did she know Gabe?

The more seconds ticked by, the more he racked his brain trying to figure this girl out. Talk about a complete mystery. Maybe that was why he could never completely forget about her. He still had nights when he wished she'd turn up in the crowd at the club. In the twelve months that had passed, he'd completed his community service hours, a framed diploma with Maggie's name hung proudly on his apartment wall, and he had even been given the okay to apply at the university again if he wanted to.

Which was debatable.

But he knew he was on his way to righting the wrongs of his past. In just two weeks, the club would be hosting the first annual Maggie Henriksen Memorial dance-a-thon with all proceeds going to the pediatric cancer ward at Sunrise Hospital. No way did Jay consider himself everything Maggie had envisioned, but he was sure as hell working on it. The thought of the benefit in his sister's honor made his eyes tear up as he focused on Kelley again. There still was no explanation for it, but there was just something about her that like Maggie, made him want to be better. And for the record, he'd never believed this angel capable of the cold last words she'd texted him. Her soul was too sweet for that.

By now she'd moved on to the next car. One he didn't recognize. Again, she rested her hand on the trunk.

Kelley's brother had sixty more seconds of his time and that was it.

He was going after her. This all felt so wrong. Screw this weird timed test Anyell seemed to need to put her through. He'd get her to agree to lunch with him and then the two of them would talk. Jay needed answers. His heart flopped over in his chest when he saw her head fall into her two hands.

Screw this. It was impossible staying there on the wrong side of the glass door. He shoved the doors open and made his way out to her.

The very last thing he expected was how desperate the look on her face was when he caught up to her.

"Please, go away. You don't want to see this."

"Kelley?" Jay looked back to see if her brother had followed him. ESPN—geez, he just couldn't seem to let go of that nickname—was there, but had stayed behind at the entrance. "Kelley, see what?"

She just blinked and looked away. His heart had no idea what to do so it sped up and thumped harder than he'd ever felt it do before. "Hey, as far as I can tell, there's nothing to see out here, right? Everything is okay. You're okay." God, he wanted to reach out and touch her, take her in his arms and hold her until she felt his strength wrap around her and she stopped with the shaking.

"You're a horrible liar." She sniffed. "I just, I came out here for some fresh air."

Yeah, and to find her car which she had yet to do. He started to ask if he could help but sensed she was really freaked out and didn't want to make it worse by embarrassing her. Jay walked a couple steps closer and reached his hand out to rub her shoulder. She dipped it, avoiding the contact, but then shot him a heartbreaking look that asked his forgiveness. God, she had it. A million times over, she had it. If he could only make her see it. He tried staring the words into her eyes but knew she didn't have the capability to read him that way yet. He decided to use his humor to put her at ease instead.

"I'm starving. You know they don't feed the help and I've usually had at least three meals by now. Let's go get something to eat. I'll drive. My car's right there." He pointed and watched her follow his finger to his Subaru. "And then I promise I'll bring you back here or drop you wherever you need to be."

She pulled down on her already long enough sleeves—sleeves which sent red flags all through his mind in this heat—and he was sure she was about to say no but something cracked through on her face, giving him a splinter of hope. God, please let her say yes, he thought. And then please don't let her brother come charging up after them and snatch her away. At that thought, he looked back toward where Anyell would be, slyly so Kelley didn't get freaked out again.

Her voice startled him but he loved hearing her speak to him. "I'm sorry, I can't. In fact, there's something I forgot to get inside, what I came here for today. I need to go back. But you should go." Her face seemed so pained. Like there was more she wasn't saying.

He was losing her again. He could feel it in his bones.

A bead of sweat dripped down the side of her face. Her look became distant. Something had her attention and he had no idea what it was. But it wasn't unreasonable that she'd be hesitant to get in a car with a relative stranger. A man at that. There he went coming on way too strong again. Something about her did that to him.

Jay looked around and found exactly what he was looking for, not willing to give up just yet. He pointed in the opposite direction of where his car was parked. "I understand, but uh, look, up there."

He made sure to smile and speak gently, having no idea what was wrong or what might upset her. It wasn't working though. She just shook her head back and forth and scratched at her black bangs hanging perfectly at her eyebrows except for the strands stuck with sweat. How in the hell was she out here in a sweater and jeans?

Not an inch of her skin was showing except her face and hands. She started to back away. He'd better act fast.

"Okay. How about this. You go back inside and take care of what you came here to do. I'm gonna walk over to that diner up there. See, that one right up there. The Coffee Mug. And when you're done, if you're feeling up to it, you come join me. Deal?" It was only a couple blocks, in plain sight from where they currently stood. Even her brother should be okay with that choice. Jay prayed she'd say yes.

"I just ca—"

He stopped her mid-word.

"You don't have to decide right now." He smiled gently. Not big and eager. Just plain and friendly. "Just think about it." And with that, he gave her a quick nod and as much as it killed him to do it, he walked off in the direction of the diner before she could start to say no again. It dawned on him that he was walking away from something special, again. Yeah, sometimes you just knew that quickly. If he could just get her to somehow see it too.

Jay walked.

At the stop light one block down, he turned back to see if she was still there. He didn't know what it meant, but even from a block away, he could see her looking in his direction, arms crossed over her midsection, before she turned and faded into the sea of cars in the shelter's lot. The light turned green and he kept on, ignoring the urge to go back and convince her to come with him. But maybe there was something to letting her decide for herself. Damn, he clenched down with his back teeth a few times then forced himself to keep walking in the direction of the diner.

"I guess we'll just wait and see," he muttered into the hot July air, begging for the patience he knew was necessary in this situation. But then a thought came to him and hope sprang up in his chest. In two weeks there was the charity dance-a-thon where all the money he made in tips would go to his sister's fund set up for the kids. It might be a horrible idea, but he just couldn't help picturing Kelley coming to the club to see the good, positive stuff he got to do as a dancer.

He glanced up to the sky.

"Mags, if you're up there, I'm asking for help. Don't let me screw this one up again. She's the one, isn't she? Yeah, I feel it too."

He then bowed his head and shuffled off the rest of the way to the diner to be something he struggled with on a daily basis. Patient.

****

"I'll see you soon, sweetheart," said Donovan to a young lady whom he'd swayed to adopt a trio of kittens today and made promise to come visit the club.

He grabbed his backpack, ready to leave the animal shelter, but not before he took care of one last thing. For as much game as his boy Jay had at the club, that game was nowhere to be found in real life. Homeboy had been all ate up—the entire year—over this chick, and she magically shows up today? Even a knucklehead like himself would have seen that as divine intervention or some crazy stuff and gotten down on one knee then and there. All that karma and universe mambo jambo was serious business you didn't screw around with. Luckily, it hadn't found him yet. D looked up to the ceiling and chewed his cheek on one side. He'd never admit it to anyone. Nope. Not even gonna think it here and now either.

"This is about Jay, dude. Not you and—" He stopped himself from even thinking her name, afraid of jinxing the poor girl he worked with. He'd only break her heart and he actually respected her way too much for that. Just then the shelter's receptionist called his name and saved his ass from the wasted thoughts.

"Hey, Donovan! Thanks again for coming today. We halfway cleared the shelter! You Club Mantasy boys rock! I wish you guys could come every weekend." She sure was cute and he got a chuckle out of her excitement. Redheads did something for him he couldn't deny, but watching Sandy and the joy her smile let out, he also knew that the one redhead he'd just been trying not to think about called to him in a different way. A way that scared him. He shook his head again trying to spare the woman whose nightly looks haunted him.

"Wow, that's great." Now was when he turned on the charm. He needed some information from a certain adoption record. "It's not us. You lovely ladies are the special ones who do all the hard work." He meant every word of it, even if he was trying to manipulate the situation.

"Um, was there anything you needed help with?" she asked him.

"You know actually, there is." D smiled. Sandy blinked a couple times. He would wager she was silently repeating the word *anything* in her mind. He quickly assessed the situation. If he wanted to be successful, he should lead with something that wouldn't put Sandy in competition with another female. That meant taking the angle that he needed to connect with a guy rather than just a lady. He thought for a moment, devising a quick excuse. "I helped a brother and sister adopt a puppy today and I know this is going to sound crazy, but the brother was interested in coming down and auditioning at the club." Yeah, so it was a bold-faced lie but as long as he wasn't hurting anyone, he didn't see it as a big deal and the guy looked a hell of a lot like Turtle. Anyways, the truth tended to fuck with people worse than a white lie. Sandy's eyes brightened. Donovan would owe her big time and knew she was about to give him what he needed. "I promised the guy I'd get in contact with him but being the complete knucklehead that I am, I let him leave without getting his info."

At the self-deprecating comment, Sandy's face took on the one that said she'd love to help him boost his self-esteem. It was one of his favorite looks.

"Oh Hon, I might get in trouble but..." Her voice lowered to a whisper and she leaned over her counter to get closer to him. "I can absolutely help you out and you shouldn't put yourself down that way. We here at the shelter think the world of you. I think you're great."

He smiled, knowing she was being genuine.

"Thank you, sweetheart."

She blushed. It was one of the most beautiful things a woman's skin could do in his opinion. But here and now, all the sight of that rosy skin did for D was remind him that the woman constantly on his mind, who he was vigilantly trying to not think of, had never blushed in his presence. Not once. D cleared his throat and acted like Sandy had been the one to distract him. He gave her a half grin and touched the tops of her hand with a gentle squeeze.

It only took a few more minutes and he was able to copy down not only a name and phone number, but the Phillips's home address. Which was perfect. Whereas D would have been all about sending a quick text invite, he knew his boy Jay would have gone and done it old school. Which meant D's next stop had to be a card store and then the post office.

"Sandy, you're a complete lifesaver. Come out to the club sometime soon. Let me make it up to you."

"I'm free tonight!" she said, nearly stumbling back down into her receptionist chair.

He winked and she giggled.

Chapter Eleven

Thirty minutes had passed and with them the dusky sky had finally given way to the night. Dark heat trapped bursts of a breeze but not enough to stay in one place and cool her down. Still, she found comfort in her long sleeves and jeans. She'd been close to hyperventilating, having practiced her deep breathing exercises too keenly and had now left the safety of her locked car and methodically steered herself to the building's entrance. Kelley pulled out the shiny red and black invitation she'd found tucked inside the puppy's official adoption paperwork that had been left on her doorstep. That day it had arrived, her world had become both complete confusion yet so singularly simple and true.

No, she hadn't made it to the diner.

She'd tried. Stood there looking in like a voyeur, mentally yelling at herself to woman up and join him. God, he'd looked so kind and handsome and welcoming. His hair had grown longer, curling more at the ends and making it to the middle of his neck. The blond had darkened and he still wore the same not quite perfect beard and mustache. She wondered if he thought it made him look older. It didn't. What did that was his eyes. To be that kind, that tolerant, that giving of themselves, a person had to have lived a lot in life, no matter what their chronological age. The life he'd lived came through in the fine lines and shadows. He'd be twenty-seven now. Still so young. Even though she was barely twenty-three, Kelley felt ancient and tired and knew that no one could understand why.

It would have meant the world to her to have been able to join him that day. To sit there in his presence, across the table from his smile, and soak in all his goodness. She even enjoyed seeing the smiles he brought to the flirty, gorgeous waitress and the hardened biker mama at the coffee bar. But there was no room for what she needed and the secret she had to keep.

So yes, she'd given herself a million reasons to go inside. It was to no avail.

Sometimes, you just knew things about people.

When Kelley looked at Jay, she could feel it deep within her soul that he wanted to get close. The worst part was how badly she wanted it too. That made it all the harder and more painful knowing she could never let that happen. That being said, the handwritten note inside the invitation about this being an evening to honor his late sister and benefit children with cancer had been impossible to ignore.

"I'll pay my respects, show my support. A polite hello," she mumbled to herself but knew how hard even those simplicities would be. Still, she vowed to do that much. For the thirty minutes of joy he'd given her all those months ago. Her mind wandered off…

Another vision of Jay sitting in that far booth off in the corner of the diner, sipping from a mug and chatting with the beautiful young waitress snapped her attention. Her ego had felt bruised for a nano-second until she'd seen that he must have asked for a second menu because the waitress returned and set the extra one down in the empty seat across from him. Yes, it could have been a seat reserved for anyone. Nothing decreed it was for her. Except she knew it was, in her heart. He'd somehow left her with no questions about that. The thing he'd done next broke her heart.

Jay sat there staring at the extra menu for long enough that when she'd had to tear herself away from the diner's glass window, he was still staring down at it.

Hopefully, her being here now would amend not being able to face him that day. Suffice it to say, a part of Kelley was terrified of what she was about to do and where she was.

Each time someone went inside, a chime sounded and Kelley's eyes scurried immediately to a small sign posted by the entrance that said, "Stay awhile and Smile." She couldn't believe she was even contemplating this as her nerves warded off any chance of a smile right now. But, this was something she had to do. She knew it with everything she had.

On a deep inhale and even stronger exhale, she put one foot in front of the other and made it happen, opening the heavy black door and entering Club Mantasy.

A gorgeous young woman with red hair, porcelain skin, and a bright pink smile motioned from the bar. "Hey Hon, welcome to S."

The personal greeting surprised Kelley, especially after a quick look around that showed plenty of other people filled the inside.

"S?" she stuttered out. In her heightened apprehension, had Kelley gotten herself to the wrong place? "I'm sorry, I was looking for Club Mantasy." Just saying the words brought out her deficiencies.

"Oh, you're in the right place," the redheaded beauty said. "We're slowly but surely changing the name out. S is for Stay, among other things." She winked and paused then wiped some glasses clean. After a moment, she wiped her hands on the front of her small black apron and then stuck out a hand. "Hi, I'm Marie. So are you meeting friends or are you the first one here? I'm usually great with faces but we've got lots of new ones tonight with the benefit and all."

"Oh, no friends." Kelley looked around, wondering if Jay was there, and found it was a bad idea to wonder such things. Seeing the club now and how dark and intimate it was both calmed and worried her. With the lights on, the space would probably look imposing but the darkened atmosphere, the colorful mood lighting, and the wait staff maneuvering about gave a sense of energy and life. Still feeling overwhelmed, Kelley took notice of a group of young ladies dressed in what she would call lingerie. One wore a sash and tiara. Covered from head to toe, she couldn't feel any more out of place. "You know, I actually think I'm gonna just step out. Sorry." She tucked her hair behind one ear several times and turned to leave, looking down mostly and hoping she'd escape without him seeing her.

"Hey. Hey, don't go. First time here, right?"

Kelley couldn't find it in herself to ignore the kind spoken woman who reminded her of dazzling yet guarded gemstones. She closed her eyes and searched for a shred of that confidence she'd had a year ago and nearly stumbled when she found it buried deep in her heart. That effervescent warmth she'd finally plugged into the few days she'd spent on her own. Later, on the last day, she remembered the smile he'd left her with. Kelley turned around.

This is exactly what you need. You can do this.

She returned her focus to Marie's shiny, ruby red waves and the gold and diamond snake necklace that wrapped around her wrist and nodded yes.

"You don't strike me as the kind of girl who's sat at many bars. Have a seat. This one's reserved for you tonight, girly. You're hangin' with me." Marie pointed to the high-backed barstool. "Come on. Sit down and I'll tell you about the first time I walked in here. There were penny-loafers involved. Brown ones," she said and then winked on a smile.

Kelley took a giant breath and let it out. "How can I say no to that?"

"Right?"

As soon as Kelley was seated, Marie patted her hand and the story began. By the end of it, she knew she'd made a girlfriend. An unprecedented novelty, it was.

"And that was two years ago?" asked Kelley.

The kind and happy look on Marie's face dimmed for a moment. "A lot can happen to a girl when she decides there's got to be something better out there. Ya know what I'm sayin'?"

"Yeah, I actually do." It was the first time Kelley had let out an honest statement about her own ordeal. Although Marie didn't go any further about a subject Kelley was sure had more to it, she felt a camaraderie had just been built. Like magic. She now had a friend.

"So, now that you're staying, I hope you plan on supporting our cause tonight," said Marie as she smiled at another patron who walked up to the bar and requested a fresh splash of seltzer water in their glass. She then turned and refilled Kelley's ginger ale.

"Oh, absolutely. That was the one thing I was definitely looking forward to doing. Will there be a collection taken up or is there someone I need to see to give my donation to?"

A mischievous grin gave Marie a dimple on one side of her face. "Oh Hon, that's not how it works here." She winked.

"No?"

Her new friend's head swiveled from side to side and she leaned over the bar and physically guided Kelley to turn with her and face one of the stages behind them. There were actually several small circular stages and one larger square one centered in the spacious room that had turned out to be quite classy looking to Kelley. From the time she'd walked in to now, she could see the stages had become rimmed with females of all ages, signaling there would be something of great interest happening on them soon. A nervous bug travelled up her insides. Now that Kelley took a moment to listen, the noise level had risen quite a bit with excited chatter.

"See those stages?" She continued, not letting Kelley answer. "Pretty soon they're gonna be filled with Boulder City's most gorgeous, talented men. The S men." Marie raised her one eyebrow two quick times.

Kelley couldn't help but interrupt. "Really? Even tonight with it being a benefit?" She didn't know what she'd thought but had envisioned more of a formal dinner setting. Maybe even a fancy, catered buffet like she'd seen at her cousin's wedding.

"Oh, especially with it being a benefit. The guys will be at their absolute best tonight. Guaranteed. But don't let that scare you off. When the time comes, we'll find you just the right gentleman to go give your donation to."

For a second, Kelley felt relief wash over her. "Oh good. I thought you were gonna say I'd have to go up there and stick, I mean stuff, I mean put it somewhere. I'm way more comfortable just handing it to someone."

Marie licked her lips and held them together for a second then shook her head but as if she was doing it in the kindest way possible. "Okay. Maybe sticking and stuffing are a bit much for your first time. Good use of S words, by the way." Marie winked again and if she didn't know any better, Kelley would have thought the slow, flicking eye movement had glammering powers because what Kelley should be doing was shaking like a frightened leaf. Each second that ticked by in Marie's presence, Kelley could feel herself becoming less traumatized. It was a miracle. What Kelley feared was that no amount of magic or faith or extremely kind people would ever be able to get her beyond where she was now. And she wanted beyond so very badly, so badly it hurt. "I tell you what, one of the guys is absolutely great with the newbies. He's super outgoing, super sweet and super sexy but not in an 'I wanna eat you for dessert' kind of way."

Instantly, Kelley became aware there would be a climate of sexiness in the air the likes she'd never experienced. She crossed her arms and whether on purpose or not, she swung her head around in a quick glance to find the exit door. She swallowed and then forced her attention back to Marie, trying to ignore the nausea.

Another wink, although this time softer, and Marie continued. "When he comes out, we'll give him a couple minutes to get used to the crowd and then I'll walk you up there to him. You can slide your tip to—."

"S-slide?" Kelley stuttered.

"Don't worry, Hon. I wouldn't set you up for failure. He is 100% gentleman. In fact, he served in the army and was awarded a pretty serious medal for getting his squad out of a very dangerous situation. He keeps quiet about that stuff because he doesn't want us fawning all over him but trust me, you won't find a sweeter guy. And the reason we have to give him a moment to warm up to the crowd is because he's shy."

True to her nature, although it had been a while, Kelley opened her mouth, intending on sounding at least somewhat pulled together. It just didn't come out that way.

"Is his name Jay?"

Marie looked as if she'd been about to respond then thought better of it, sealing her mouth with a closed smile. "Jay? That flirt doesn't have a shy bone in his body although he is very sweet too and a perfect gentleman."

Not a shy bone anywhere in his body? Maybe there were two Jays who danced here. Kelley had thought one of her Jay's most endearing qualities was how he seemed to mirror her awkwardness, something she chalked up to him being shy. Kelley didn't know how to respond and so she stayed quiet.

"I'm sorry, Hon. Do you know Jay? I just, I didn't even think with you being a newbie and all. Jay's great, by the way. Super nice guy. You should have said you know him." Marie could have made Kelley feel like a fraud but she never did. She just kept on with their friendly, girly banter and her soft smiles all the while tending to bar patrons. "Give me a second and I'll go get him for ya."

"Oh no! No, don't."

"Okay, okay." Marie's kind face scrunched up as soon as Kelley freaked out on her with the no's. "Hmm, I gotta tell ya, Hon. You are a mysterious one, even more than me."

And then it all started gushing out...

"I'm so sorry. It's just that I only met him once, a year ago. And then I randomly adopted a dog from him a couple weeks ago. I guess part of the pet adoption must have come with an invitation to this benefit tonight. That's the only reason I mentioned his name or even knew about tonight. I would be so embarrassed if you went and got him for me. It's not like that. I'm no one special to him. At all."

She'd been telling herself that for so long now. The barrier she'd put up with those words was just safer. Although, being here tonight, in his surroundings, she could admit her curiosity. But only to herself. Only ever to herself.

"I totally gotcha. No worries then. Well, I still think Gabe is your best bet for tipping. But hey, when Jay comes out, I bet he'd get a kick out of seeing you. He's one of those who never forgets a face and with one as pretty as yours, there's no way he's forgotten you from the adoption event. Your hair is great, by the way. I wish I could get my bangs to behave like yours. And, if you're feeling wild and crazy after this next ginger ale, maybe I'll even be able to convince you to tip them both. After all, it's for a good cause!"

"Oh boy," she said.

"Hahahaha. I like you, Kelley. You just wait and see. Before tonight's over, we'll have you sliding and sticking and stuffing with the best of them. And you're in luck because there's Gabe taking the stage. Got your money handy? You're in for a real treat with this number."

Treat? Oh dear lord, what did that mean? Marie pointed out one of the most physically flawless looking men Kelley had ever seen. Softly tanned and dressed in a white naval officer's uniform with the spotlight hanging over him from above, he glowed like an angel.

"Come on, let's go watch him up close. Brad, watch the bar for me, please?"

A young, hip looking man with a tie and vest and lip piercing nodded at her.

One last wink from Marie and Kelley's stomach flip-flopped. They joined hands and Marie tugged Kelley up to the edge of the stage.

"Marie, I think I'm going to throw up."

"Shh, no you won't. Just breathe in, now breathe out, hear the music and focus on his movements."

Kelley did as Marie suggested, grateful Marie hadn't left her side. Gabe walked like he'd been born on the stage yet he had this underlying demeanor that told her he really was very shy, just as Marie had said. The contradiction worked to mesmerize her for the moment. This went way beyond what she'd intended for tonight. Kelley inhaled another deep breath and watched his face and the softness of his expressions. He seemed to smile at each person individually and mouthed the words "hello" and "thank you" to those who waved and hollered at him. She had immediate respect for the kind man.

"I can do this," she chanted and watched, focusing on refined, tanned fingers slowly pulling apart the front opening of the officer's coat. She had to glance down at the sight of his bare chest.

"Yes, you can," said Marie before waving at the dancer named Gabe.

Kelley's throat became dry as if she hadn't been sipping liquid the past half hour. A lump threatened to choke her out. Before she knew it, the tall, dark and handsome man went from standing to kneeling right in front of her. It felt like all eyes must be on the two of them. Talk about daunting. Afraid to look at him this close up and with no idea what to do, she kept her head turned to the side, avoiding it all. She heard Marie's voice.

"Gabe, this is Kelley. It's her first time at the club, or any club for that matter, and she's here to support Maggie's Benefit."

Kelley felt a large, warm hand wipe softly over the top of the fingers of her left hand and then cup them. Fighting instinct, she refused to flinch. He was kind. She knew this after two seconds in his presence. "Hello, Kelley, it's nice to meet you." He was then quiet for several seconds.

Turn your head. Turn your head!

She felt his grip loosening up and knew she already owed him an apology for acting so strange. Speaking and turning to look at him at the same time, she said with as much voice as she could muster. "I'm sorry my hands are so sweaty. I've also been drinking tons of ginger ale and I really could use a trip to the ladies room."

That made him chuckle quietly while all Kelley wanted to do was go hide under a table.

"Oh my God, I'm so sorry. I have this public speaking problem—" she started to say but the man, Gabe, cut her off.

"You should feel my hands right now. Go ahead," he spoke, leaning into her ear so she could hear him better and his breath tickled her skin. He stuck his hands out palm up and Kelley hesitated but then wiped at them.

"Holy cow, they really are!"

Gabe looked to Marie and they laughed together.

"She's adorable, right? Remind you of anyone?" said Marie to Gabe.

"Mr. Henriksen," the two said in unison.

"Mr. Henriksen? Who is that? The club owner?" Kelley's head swam.

"Not quite," said Marie with a grin. "Dancer."

"Speak of the devil," said Gabe which seemed to catch Marie's attention and funny bone at the same time as she let out a small, chirpy laugh.

Kelley wasn't ready to focus on yet another half-clothed, drop-dead gorgeous man and she remembered that she wanted to make a donation. She reached in her small purse and pulled out her two twenty dollar bills. She knew it wasn't much, but it was all the extra money she had this month. Not feeling like she'd be able to handle meeting anyone else and content to spend the rest of the night watching from afar, she handed the two twenties to Gabe. Plus, there was just no way she could imagine exchanging money in this way with Jay should she actually get to see him tonight.

Gabe reached for her hand and kissed the tops of her knuckles, somehow keeping her fingers cupped so her money didn't fall from her hand.

"I'm honored, little mama," he said, his voice low and sultry but completely friend-like. "But you might want to cash this out for some singles and spread it around. It might be more fun for you that way." He leaned down again, close to her ear and whispered the rest. "I promise you're safe here and I get it's your first time. We're all here to take care of you."

"Um, no, I just want to give it to you if that's okay." Kelley couldn't see herself hanging around at the front of the stage for much longer and was sure her security blanket, Marie, would have to go back to her post at the bar soon. When that happened, Kelley would lose what little motivation she had to be acting so bravely. More importantly, she remembered that a certain blond-haired man would be coming out eventually and she needed to be as far away as possible now that she knew from seeing Gabe what Jay would most likely be doing. She wasn't ready for that.

"You sure?"

She just nodded her head up and down and tried not to pass out.

"Okay, well thank you so much. I'm humbled to be your first. Would you like to do me the honor of placing my first tip of the night where it belongs?" He slowly pivoted, offering her his hip.

She couldn't think straight. A wonderful flash of happiness and joy warmed her in ways she'd never known but out of nowhere, gnashing and sharp cutting pain felt like it tore at her skin. She silently pleaded for it to go away but it had come and whether it stayed or left, it made its point. She wasn't healed. Was that something she'd ever be able to call herself? She prayed night and day for it to happen.

"I'm sorry. I'm sorry, I can't. Here, please take it. I appreciate how kind you've been to me but no, I just would rather not put it there."

Gabe seemed to understand and offered her a genuine and warm look of complete acceptance and took the two bills she offered him into his hand. "Hey, it's okay. It's okay. Thank you for your generosity. Hey, don't worry about it. I hope you'll watch the rest of the show."

She nodded that she would and he stayed kneeled down for the time being. Marie had apparently had to run back to the bar but Kelley saw her coming up in her peripheral, sparkling as she neared. Only she wasn't alone. A man with broad, bare shoulders, suspenders and blond, neck-length hair followed at her side.

Chapter Twelve

"Hey Jay-Jay, whatcha doin'?"

Marie was acting awfully strange, playful almost. That wasn't her norm and it caught Jay's attention immediately. Had Donovan gone and finally had a serious talk with her? Maybe cut all the bs and come clean about how he felt? Jay hoped so. But now wasn't the time to play cupid. It was Maggie's Benefit night and he would be going on stage tonight to hopefully make lots of smiles and in turn, receive lots of cause-worthy tips.

"Hello, Marie. You seem happy."

"I'm always happy." She frowned.

No she wasn't. Not deep down where it counted. Jay knew that much. But she did have a certain up-beat outlook that felt fresher.

"Correction. Happy-er."

Another rarity, she cut into a huge smile.

"What are you not telling me, Miss Marie?"

"Come with me," she said.

"Where?"

"Out front."

"I'm not on yet. Gabe's up. Then Jules. Then D. I'm actually last tonight." He stopped himself from referring to D as *her man*, because he knew it was something the two might not even be aware of themselves.

"I know."

Jay normally spent as much time out front chatting with the guests as he did on stage performing for them but right now he wanted a few extra quiet moments alone to let the importance of tonight sink in.

"Jay, come."

Having thought that, Marie was rarely persistent with him like this. So he followed her out front, forgetting for the time being that he was only half-dressed for his solo. He ran his hand over his abs, rubbing away some of the sweat already sticking to his skin. He'd barely crossed paths with Julian but the bump-in had been enough and he had the man's angel wing glitter all over his black pants. Jay dusted it off as best he could, eventually giving up. Jay hooked his thumbs in his suspenders. He left the newsboy hat that would—pardon the pun—cap off his college prep outfit in homage to Maggie, in his locker and followed Marie out front. One thing he recognized for sure was the extra pep in her step. If he didn't know better, he'd have thought she was playing Cupid or something ridiculous like that. Too bad he couldn't just tell her he'd officially taken his heart off the market, for good, two weeks ago when he'd been stood up again by the girl who had somehow taken his everything prisoner.

"Yes, ma'am," he said and followed her out, pumping himself up for the night and walking to the beat of Gabe's solo song.

"So you guys had a pretty successful adoption event at the last shelter drive?"

"Yes, Marie. Why do you ask? You sure are talking to me a whole lot tonight. I mean, I love it. But, do you swear everything is okay with you?" He'd do anything he could to help her. She worked hard and he knew she had issues she kept hidden. Jay knew how that could eat at a person.

"I'm in the mood to do some good and you think there's something wrong with me? Gee, thanks, Stud."

He wasn't sure exactly what to say back to her, to be honest. It was tricky with Marie because Jay knew he had to keep his flirting to a minimum, remembering how wrecked it had made him when D had gotten too loose with his flirty words for Kelley. "My apologies to the lady."

They walked single file through the last bits of the cramped back hallways until they got to the door that led into the public portion of the club. Jay took an extra-long step to put him in front of Marie so that he could get the door for her. He ushered her through but then noted how she quickly jumped back in front of him. Guess she really wanted to be the leader.

"Accepted. And you're right, it is odd that I'm feeling so chipper. It's freaking me out but I'm going with it for this night only. I just feel like this burst of goodness came inside earlier. Apparently your sister's spirit of positivity has its claws in me tonight." She winked and smiled softly at him. "Anywho, recognize anyone?"

Marie suddenly stopped walking when they'd only made it a few feet into the club, clearly waiting for him to stop too and have a look around. Okay, he'd play along and checked out the bar area since that was where he associated Marie as being most often. "Drunk Al. Tina and her mom and her sisters. Um, Brad?" He noted the faces he could see this far in the dark.

"Ahem." She cleared her throat and pulled him around by the suspender until he was facing the stage. She let go and the elastic snapped his skin. It didn't really hurt but he let out a yelp just to tease her. "Ouch."

Now he did see a ton of familiar faces. "Do you really want me to start naming everyone? Cause there's Liz, Kerri, Dana, Kim, Alethea, Pintip, Susan, Loni, Masha, and Denny, just for starters." It gave him an immense feeling of joy that so many of the regulars were already here supporting the cause. "Oh, and let's see … Lynne, Robin, and Avery. I can keep going—Jen, Keely,

Deb, Denise, Sue, Lil. Ooo, Becky's looking supa-hot tonight. She turned fifty in here last week, you know. Still fricking gorgeous. Did you know she's the drummer in a band? I think I'm going to give her a late birthday lick later on. In fact, I think I'm gonna go over there with my sexy self and lick her right now." Of course he was just teasing, watching Marie's face get more and more perturbed with him. It was his playful payback to her for bringing him out before he'd gotten dressed and then being so secretive. But honestly, who did she want him to see?

"Ugh. You're impossible. And you wonder why I don't talk much to you boys. Gabe—"

But she may as well have stopped speaking.

The second he changed his line of sight to the stage where Gabe currently held court as a half-dressed military hero, he saw the one thing he never would have expected, not in a million years at this point.

She didn't even have to turn around for him to know.

The insides of his bones were testifying right now that it was her, his angel, his Kelley. He felt strong and weak at the same time. In a word, speechless.

"Kelley," he whispered in her direction.

"Yes, Kelley," said Marie. She patted his shoulder then tugged down on it. He gave her his ear quickly, already feeling the pull to go be near the other half of his magnet self. Apparently, this girl constantly leaving him hanging would never override the joy his soul felt whenever she was near. "She was too shy to admit it, but there's no question in my mind, she's here for you, Jay-Jay."

But before Marie even finished her sentence, he was making his way to *her*. He had only a few steps to question the black sweater dress she wore over a pair of casual jeans that ended at brown leather boots. It was the middle of summer. She'd left her shiny black hair down. His heart thumped so hard in his chest.

There could only be one reason she was here tonight. Did he dare accept that she'd finally come to see him?

"Excuse me, miss," he said and touched her softly at the small of her back.

Every muscle she had there tensed under his touch. That should have been his sign to remove his hand but he didn't want to. He was done pulling away from her. Done letting her slip out from his grasp.

It took her a second, but she turned to see who had touched her and called her miss.

Once she was looking at him, he saw it. Everything she wanted but for whatever reason hadn't been able to share with him. *It's okay,* he wanted to tell her. *You don't have to say it. I know.*

She started to blurt something out and as badly as he wanted to hear it, because her awkward bursts were the most adorable things on God's green earth, he shushed her by putting his finger gently over her lips. Yes, he would be bold with her. Jay sensed she needed it, as much as it seemed to overwhelm her whenever he did it. Part of her came alive for him when he was this way with her. Her eyes widened to double their size so he smiled.

"Me first. Okay?" He questioned her with his eyes.

She nodded okay, that he could speak first. Jay found her two hands and held them in his although hers were balled up and he felt a tremble in them. He left them like that for now and cupped her small fists into his hands.

"I cannot tell you how pleased I am that you are standing here in front of me right now." He scanned her eyes and found that they were glued to his. Trusting that she was seeing how serious he was, he continued. "Whatever has been going on for the past year, I want you to know that it's okay. If you want to tell me, I'm all ears. If you don't want to tell me, that's perfectly fine too. I just want you to stay, right here, with me. For the next five minutes, I just need you not to leave." It took all Jay had not to let the enormous amount of emotions he was feeling out.

A beautiful yet hurting frown gave her a deep vee between her eyes. God, her eyes were so beautiful. But they also let him know that she was without question holding something inside. Something that confused her, worried her, his angel.

"I'm scared."

Oh God, he was right. Jay couldn't help but squeeze her, not sure of what she feared but praying it wasn't him. "Don't be."

It was like they were lost in their own little world, one where he would protect her no matter what. So many things he wanted to say to her went unsaid because he had to devote all his energy to seeing her, believing she was there, and trusting she wasn't going anywhere. Finally though, Gabe hopped down off the stage, tips flowing from the sides of his briefs, and walked up to Jay.

"These belong to her. Clearly they were meant for you. Good luck, bro," said Gabe in that quiet trademark voice of his so that only Jay could hear. His friend passed him two folded up bills and then left them.

Jay barely heard his friend as Motor's "Man Made Machine" blared in the background. A crazy, booming burst of females gasping the word "Whoa" bounced off the walls. The room went totally dark until a single spotlight pointed toward the ceiling where his man Julian stood on a perch. The loud ohs and ahs soared to a new level of excited now as Julian and his angel wings did a back flip onto the stage. Glitter flew from his costume, dusting the crowd. Jay had no idea how he landed it every time but he did. And that was why Jules was part of the show. Something for everyone. More screams added to the pandemonium.

Jay continued staring straight into Kelley's eyes. She hadn't looked away for even a second which made his pride soar higher than Julian's gravity defying act.

"Thank you."

"For what?" she asked, her brows rising and her forehead crinkling.

He'd tell her later what a gift it was knowing that she only had eyes for him. Right now he had about thirty minutes until it would be his turn to take the stage, having chosen to go last in the lineup for the special occasion.

"I'm going to insist you trust me right now."

"Wha?"

"Just say yes," he said.

"Yes."

His heart did that racing thing again and he held out his hand to her. It took her a couple moments, but she took it.

Thank God, she took it.

He wanted to kiss her, then and there. What lesson had his year of knowing Kelley taught him if it wasn't to act now.

Don't wait, a voice inside his head said and he could have sworn it was Maggie.

Don't wait.

He wanted to scream back at the voice that he wasn't going to wait but he would always take his time with her.

"Wait," he ended up saying.

She questioned him with her eyes. His stomach clenched in anticipation. He reached up and stroked her cheek and the hair falling against it. Both were so soft. The softest things he'd ever felt.

"Jay, what is happening?" she asked.

He gently guided her to the nearest wall then turned her around so that she faced him. He could see in her eyes that she was nervous, maybe because she was the one with the view of the entire club at their backs while his eyes had the pleasure of only seeing her.

"I feel like I'm constantly about to lose you. I can tell you need time but I've been waiting so long to do this." She looked confused while his mouth watered just to have his lips touching hers. This close, she smelled like one of his favorite places, the grocery store aisles where you could smell the baby powder and the fresh flowers together. Such sweet things had never given him such explicit thoughts but there was no denying it.

His body surged with raw, tender desire.

Like nothing he'd ever wanted before, he wanted to be inside her, under and on top of her, surrounding her.

He wanted to share his body with her but also his heart and his thoughts. Afraid that if he asked permission to kiss her, she'd say no, he leaned in and angled his head down so that his forehead rested against hers. For one more moment, he thought about what he was about to do. She didn't try to move out from under him. She wasn't saying no. If the earth stopped existing just then, this would be enough. How was it that he could feel so much satisfaction from the smallest of touches?

Trailing the fingers of his right hand up the back of her neck, through all that thick, gorgeous black hair, Jay held her face in place so that he could finally touch his lips to hers.

"I will always take my time with you." He had to whisper that to her.

As soon as they connected in this way, it felt amazing.

Until he realized she'd gone cold and still as a stone.

"Hey, Kelley." He shook her gently but all he could see was a lost little girl in her big green eyes. "Angel, are you okay?"

****

Tell him. You are okay. Tell him now, Kelley. Come on, don't do this. Not now. Pull it together. You are okay, say it.

She couldn't tell him what had happened a year ago. She couldn't explain to him why she was so strange and awkward. She could never let him find out what had happened to her. But right now, she could accept a kiss.

"I am okay. Kiss me, Jay."

****

His eyes widened and his forehead crinkled in surprise but then he leaned in and kissed her sweetly on the cheek. "You have no idea how long I've waited to hear you say that."

"Oh, I have an idea."

He couldn't help but chuckle and used her mouth opening into a small smile as the icebreaker for a kiss on her delectable lips. He loved that her lips were completely natural with no make up to get in the way. When she gasped, he felt it on his lips and then she did something that broke his heart but also let him know she trusted him. Or at least she wanted to trust him. The saltiness of a tear dripped down her cheek. When he pulled away from the gentle exploring of her mouth to press his lips to her cheek and the tear, she let out a huge breath and her tiny frame fell into his chest.

He held her firmly to him and she began to whisper. It was so hard to hear her in the club but he was using all his concentration.

"Jay, I'm so scared right now, so broken. I should be running away and not looking back."

"No, you absolutely should not be doing that," he said as he stroked her hair. "Please promise me you won't do that."

"I didn't say it's what I want to do. But it would be the kind thing to do—"

He stopped her mid-sentence. That made no sense. "What do you mean? I want a chance with you, Kelley. Stay with me, let me try."

She blinked several times, he felt the flutter of her eyelashes on his chest. "I mean that I'll frustrate you to no end. I know because I do it to myself. Every day. I'm afraid I'll be more trouble than I'm worth, Jay. It'll get old. Fast." She looked up at him and their eyes met and locked. "There's a reason for all this. And it's something I'll never talk about. No matter how safe I feel with you, no matter how much I trust you, there are parts of me I'll never be able to share. How could you want that?"

He considered everything she'd just said to him. How did he make her understand there was just something inside him that let him know even with all that, they were meant to be in each other's lives? He wanted to prove himself to her, that he could handle it. That he was meant to help her. It was the only explanation for their paths crossing. The joy he felt at discovering this knowledge and feeling so strongly about it, so determined, left him with a rush and a high. He'd never been surer of anything in his life. The fact that this was all happening on such a special night was the icing on the cake. He had to take a breath.

"I just know."

"You just know?"

"Yep," he said matter of factly as people continued doing their thing all around the protected bubble that was his and Kelley's private corner space.

She seemed to consider that short answer for a moment.

"Okay. But promise me one thing, please."

"Anything."

"When I get stuck. When I pull away and it seems like I'm being selfish or stubborn and I can't let go of my secrets, promise you won't take it personally."

It was so much to take in and he was very aware that he was committing to a lot of very serious and heavy stuff, but he'd do anything she asked. "I promise, Angel." He then took her face in his two hands and left kisses at her forehead, nose, lips and chin.

Jay looked up when he felt a fist bump against his shoulder. Instinctively, he wrapped Kelley in his arms, shielding her from his visitors.

D, along with Gabe and Jules, walked by giving him nods and smiles. When they'd passed, he loosened up his embrace so she could see something besides his biceps again.

"Jay, one more thing."

"Anything. Always, anything."

She glanced down at their feet before looking back up into his eyes. Hers had become shinier. "Never ask to see my skin."

A tear leaked from her eyes and it filled him with her heartbreak. Jay knew he'd just promised not to push her, but part of wanting a relationship with Kelley meant helping her past whatever had just caused one of the shyest girls he knew to be so bold and honest. The enormity of what he was committing to hit him like a ton of bricks.

Like he said earlier, for her, he'd do anything.

One of these days, he'd get her past this.

He'd show her that she could open up and let him see whatever it was that had her so afraid.

"I promise."

"Then I guess my answer is yes."

"Wait, what was the question? Did I ask you something? I don't recall," he said with a sly grin, fingers crossed it got the effect he craved.

Slowly, her lips curved into the most gorgeous, glorious smile.

"You're a real brat, you know that?" Man, he loved how she teased him right back.

Jay rubbed at his whiskers and bit his bottom lip for her then wagged his eyebrows. "I'm your brat."

"Oh my God," she said. "I've never had a boyfriend, you know."

"Yeah, oh my God," he said, loving the glow her face got when she smiled like that. He couldn't wait to see her expression when he took her backstage right now for a quick lesson.

Jay took her smaller hands in his and began escorting her to the private quarters.

"Where are we going?" she asked but kept moving along with him.

"You're dating a stripper, Angel. You need to learn how to leave him a proper tip." She stopped. He turned and winked and moved his hands to her hips and squeezed, making her jump. "So when do I get to meet Mom and Dad?" For a second he worried that he'd just blown it, asking about parents he didn't know if she had. They could have passed or been estranged.

He watched her swallow but in true Kelley fashion, she didn't disappoint. "That's awfully ambitious. Probably should wait and see if you survive telling Anyell first."

They hugged and it fired his body's every nerve and cell, reminding him of the promise he'd made to honor her strange request. She didn't want him to see her skin. Skin he remembered as being so beautiful and radiant on their walk. Skin he'd dreamed of kissing inch by slow inch.

He had the thought that tomorrow they should sit down over breakfast and have a conversation about what she was comfortable with beings that she'd been very clear on what she was not okay with. The thought of not being able to gaze at and appreciate her beauty hurt, but could he touch her? Hold her in his arms and kiss her? There was so much to figure out.

"What's that smirk about?" she asked him as they made their way to the back and now stood by his locker. "You're already re-thinking things, aren't you? It's okay. I don't blame you."

Jay took her chin in his hand, intending to assure her that he was committed to her but she immediately jerked it away. Her eyes turned so sad and she looked down. He'd done something wrong. Triggered something that had to do with that bad secret.

"Kelley, I'm so sorry."

"Me too. I told you this was going to be hard."

"Hey, I'm not going anywhere. I care about you so much. You are worth it."

"You say that now. But what about in a week, or a month from now?"

"I'll have learned so much about you by then, it'll get better. You'll see. I'll adjust. It'll be fine. We'll be fine." He decided he wasn't giving up for anything and pulled her to him in another tight hug then slowly and gently allowed his hands to caress her back up and down as he continued to hold her. She was stiff at first but settled into the soothing motion.

"See? I'm a fast learner," he said and concentrated on her muscles that still felt tight with tension under his hands. God, how he enjoyed the sensation of being able to provide for her like this. The material of her sweater bunched under his fingers as he pressed and soothed. He was now beginning to understand more about why she dressed in such warm weather clothes in the middle of summer. She was hiding something underneath.

"No, what you are is an angel," she said.

His heart soared. He thought of her that way but never thought to ever be called someone's angel. A small smile took up on his face and he knew it was for Mags. A tear leaked out from his eye but before he could wipe it away, Kelley reached up and did that for him.

"I haven't felt hope in a very long time, Jay. Tonight, it's here. Everywhere inside me. You are a gift. And I'm going to do everything I can to cherish that. I pray that I don't hurt your feelings while we're figuring things out."

"Hope is a good thing."

"Yes, it is." She chewed at her lip in a nervous way and then did something so brave, he nearly pulled a Kelley and blurted how much he loved her there on the spot. But she stunned him when she said, "I hope that someday I'm a stronger person. And that I can one day have the courage to let you see me. I can't promise anything, but I will try."

The air whooshed out of his lungs and there was no stopping either of their tears. One by one, they fell. Jay had never cried in public like this, couldn't believe he was doing it now.

"Hey you," she said. "Good luck out there tonight."

Searching her eyes, he tried transferring all his emotions into her soul through his gaze.

"Thank you, Kelley. That means a lot."

"I know. I can tell. For the record, I'm proud of who you are and what you do. And I look forward to the day when I get to introduce you to my parents."

That touched him so much. Jay wished he could stand back there talking to her like this for the rest of the night but it was his time to go perform. With his hand over his heart, he rubbed at the spot and blew her a kiss. "You coming?"

"I wouldn't miss it for the world. I can't believe I have a boyfriend. And you're so totally hot. It's just crazy!"

They both laughed. It was great!

Part of their breakfast conversation was going to have to include what things like that did to him when she said them. His parting thought before heading out to the stage was the bittersweet longing of making love to Kelley. He honestly didn't know if that was a possibility for them. When he realized in that second that it wasn't a deal breaker, Jay couldn't help himself.

"No, what's crazy is how much I love you." It was so loud. He had no idea if she'd heard him. That was okay. It kind of felt like he'd have more chances in the very near future.

He winked and walked out to the stage.

****

Oh dear God, please help me be what he needs. Please, if I get one answered prayer in my lifetime, let this be the one.

Kelley let him go ahead of her, hanging back for just a few moments. Her fingers hovered over her lips. "He loves me," she whispered to herself and then to him, although he was too far ahead to hear. "He really loves me."

"Yes he does." The familiar face from the adoption event popped into her view. He wore nothing but sweat and a thong. "Donovan, by the way. But you can call me D." He smiled a sparkling white smile that made her blush although she sensed she owed this man something. "Big ole softy has loved you for oh, I'd say about a year now." He leaned in closer. "It's really nice to see you two together. But Kelley, do me a favor."

The way he said her name, it was like he'd known her for a very long time.

"Okay," she said, feeling an awareness of a bond Jay must have with this man and wanting to honor that.

"If the day comes that you have to break his heart, be quick and final about it.

Chapter Thirteen

Two months later, September...

Evidently, two could *not* play this game.

So angry she nearly cried, Kelley sucked back the tears soaking her throat which kept her from screaming for him.

They'd made it for two months, and God did she love this man, but it had been trial and error from the start. Which was why she'd been so reluctant about staying the night for the first time. His bed might still be warm from where they'd just been cuddling in it.

Maybe after tonight, it was best her parents hadn't made it home yet to meet him.

There was so much he'd miss out on were he to commit to her and only her and that wasn't fair. She was proving it right now.

Rubbing hard circles against her eyes with the heels of her damp palms, Kelley had to consider the possibility this was the hard evidence that she and Jay just weren't compatible. His gorgeous smile flashed in her mind. The dimpled one he always got whenever they met and he first spied her coming toward him. He was wanted by so many. God, that first time she'd seen him at the club. It was his smile and the way he walked around with such confidence and joy in each step he took. How she'd managed to snag him was still a mystery. She didn't want to lose him. Not after everything she'd done to get herself at least this well, this healed. Enough to function as his angel as he always called her.

He was her happy.

Except for not right now. Not if he'd done what she suspected. She glanced around the bathroom a second time. It was bare.

Her face contorted as if she needed to sob just as much as she needed to breathe. Both came out in pinches and made an ugly sound. Her hands flew to her mouth to keep it from happening again. She waited a few seconds and when she felt in control, at least enough, she swallowed and cleared her throat a final time. It was cold. She was wet.

She rung water from her hair, tugging it over her shoulder and squeezing so the droplets fell into his tub. She stepped out from the shower and tiptoed across his bathroom floor in search of a towel somewhere. She checked the cupboard under the sink but all she found there was extra rolls of toilet paper and his shaving kit. Crazy, but there had been towels when she first entered the shower, hadn't there?

Now, there were none, anywhere.

Had he snuck in here while she showered and stolen them all? That's what she feared.

She searched once more in case newbie nerves were what had her blinded, but no, being here for the first time had nothing to do with it. His bathroom was simple and uncluttered. A towel, or her clothes, would stand out amongst the one bottle of cologne, the stick of deodorant and the electric toothbrush hanging out by the sink.

Jay, her tender and economical, but prank-loving boyfriend, had overstepped. He might still have his footing, but to make room, so he wouldn't fall, she'd gone off the ledge.

Water droplets that the dry Nevada air filtering through his apartment hadn't taken care of dripped down. Her front half blurred by in the bathroom mirror as she moved to kill the lights, but the view stopped her cold anyway before she made it there.

Her naked body hung in limbo as she stood there paralyzed.

Her hands fumbled over her stomach and over her ribs the same way they always did when she was forced to stop and look.

Her scars were hideous.

One tear took its time. She felt it slowly fall.

Finally it hung just below her cheek bone. That was when she wiped at it fast and hard then jammed the tip of her thumbnail deep into the groove between her two front bottom teeth.

She pushed down hard until the nail was wedged good and tight.

"Kelley, take a breath," she whispered. This was not the end of the world. "He didn't mean anything by it." She pinched the bridge of her nose and repeated that again, silently this time. "He hasn't seen anything. He's just trying to get you to open up to him more."

Kelley closed her eyes tight and breathed another hard set of tears back in through her nose. As her fingers moved over each one separately, she started a silent count of the marks, remembering how she'd received them.

One as I fell, two against the car, three before the choking...

Her breath hitched and her fingers traced over the most prominent welt. That one always brought back the worst memory and she lost count.

One, two, three, she began again, this time avoiding touching that hardest one where the skin rippled the worst, having healed poorly.

But not touching it didn't matter. She still saw it. Sometimes she hugged herself and crumpled to the floor but this time Kelley tried using the steps she'd read in her book. Slowly and with great focus and determination and her back planted firmly against the bathroom wall, she repeated until she could really hear herself. "I am taking my pieces back. I am using them to rebuild me. I am whole and here and real. With all of my pieces, I am strong."

"Kell. Lee. Oh, Kelley, I'll still want you even if you come out of there looking like a prune. You take a long shower, woman."

Surely he heard the silence biting back at him. Kelley gritted her teeth so as not to shout at him that she would have been out by now had there been any towels to dry off with.

"Thank you, by the way. For coming tonight," he said. His voice dropped an octave lower and she knew this was sincere Jay. "When do I get you back on this side of the door? Guess who doesn't look like a prune? Guess who just did sixty-five pushups just for you?"

His shoulders. The perfectly strong forces that were Jay's shoulders told her to put her hand on the doorknob, turn it, and walk with haste into his arms.

"No," she mumbled to herself.

If she opened the bathroom door, he would see it and he knew the deal.

"I will never let him see," she said, and glanced up, staring herself down in the mirror. Kelley's fingers instinctively rose to her eyebrows and she rubbed along the soft hairs from the center out. Repeatedly, she did this, finally closing her eyes again.

A soft series of taps sounded at the door. "Enjoy your shower, baby? You sure I can't join you?" His voice came slow and deep through the door. He could be so tender.

She squeezed her eyes even tighter. So tight, she felt the cartilage of her ears somehow contract. Sadness rippled over the hard lines of her scars. No, a shower together would never happen. No matter how eager her heart allowed her to feel at the prospect. Her body held her back, reminding Kelley what a selfish, horrible decision it had been to agree to stay the night tonight. Sending mixed messages wasn't her style but that's exactly what she'd done. When she found her clothes, she would extract herself and apologize and then wait for the inevitable break-up. Why should he stick around? Just because she wanted him to?

Motivated to keep Jay from seeing her, she slung her hand out toward the wall and her fingers were just long enough to kill the light switch before she answered him. Her body fell heavily against the door and she slumped. Chill bumps looked magnified under the water droplets as she rubbed her arms.

"Kelley?"

His voice was so powerful, even dulled through the thin wood. Her voice was temporarily lost to the memory of being tucked between his legs, and folded into his arms although she'd been sure to keep his hands latched with hers and away from her midsection. His constant efforts to caress her there had kept her on her toes tonight. She remembered the darkness of his room, he'd agreed to it.

Jay's body would again warm hers now if she went to him, she knew it would. His whispers were just as intoxicating now as they'd been an hour ago.

Her ear tingled, re-hearing his soft and constant chants.

How are we doing? I'm so proud of you for coming tonight. You are such a brave woman. But then his hand had reached up under her pajama top and the second his finger had met skin, she'd grabbed onto him and pushed it back to her thigh.

"Yo, hot stuff. You okay in there?" he called to her now through the door, his humor begged her to smile.

Instead, she smeared her lower lip to the side, chewing at it as she went, thinking of his attentiveness, and how badly she wished she could appreciate it. Kelley tucked into herself, trying to hide as much skin as was possible by bowing her shoulders inward and drawing her knees together, so afraid he would somehow get inside and see her scars in the light.

She should say something.

"Jay. You shouldn't have." Who knew if he heard her, with such a meek voice. What was she going to do? How was she going to get out of here without finally having to go into hideous detail about everything? At this point, he had to be out there seriously contemplating having invited her over tonight. For that matter, he probably regretted ever flirting with her that day on their walk.

A couple more soft and zingy raps at the door zipped along like a song, fitting Jay's goofy personality perfectly, and she took a second to remember that he didn't know specifically what had her hiding out in his bathroom rather than clambering back into his bed for more snuggling and footsy. He'd asked her for the specifics the one time about a month ago now, the first time when they'd really gone for it and made out in the bathroom at the club and she'd turned out the lights, and he'd kept flicking them back on. And then she'd reaffirmed that it was darkness or nothing. "I'm just kissing you," he'd said. Her lip had quivered and she'd raised her shoulders and eyebrows at the same time. He'd turned the light switch back off and engulfed her into his chest for a long hug.

She hated being this worked up over his silly prank just now but that was the thing. Jay knew better.

He'd promised he was okay with taking things at a turtle's pace.

But he was human and maybe he was finally over it. Kelley didn't picture his deep blue eyes or the curls of his long hair. His perfect dancer's body steered clear of her mind, all except for his shoulders. Strong, like pillars, she craved pressing her face into them and hiding. And she would have if he hadn't just done what he'd done. Snuck in and stolen her clothes while she showered, and every single towel down to the wash cloths. Thank God he had a solid shower curtain. She glanced at the loosely hanging plastic and shuddered. A pinch of acid lodged in her throat as she thought of what a sad shield it made.

Tonight, he'd crossed the line and sexiest, most kind man she'd ever met or not, she was pissed. So dang pissed.

"Open up so I can give you your towel," came his voice, the one she loved because of the many smiles it had brought to her face. Although this time she hissed at how easy it was for him to sway her to his side. The hint was there, telling her he was still feeling playful and nowhere near ready to actually close his eyes and go to sleep. His eyes. So intense and intelligent. She could almost feel his famished gaze through the cold, hard door. Her skin pinched as she dragged her front half over it, breasts and tummy skin sticking to the white painted wood.

A few hours ago, she'd been excited too over their first sleepover.

Things had gone so well up until fifteen minutes ago when he'd let her out of his bed to make her way in the dark to his bathroom for a shower. She never would have even considered bathing anywhere but her own home but she had to be at her teaching internship tomorrow and it was a baby step she'd tried to take tonight.

Kelley bit down and blew out, doing everything she could not to be mean to him. "And my clothes," she said through tight lips. "Just leave everything there on the floor. I swear, Jay. Don't push me right now. I don't want to fight." God, how she wanted to crawl back to him, to his bed and the sweet way he'd been holding and snuggling up behind her.

A thought filled her with sadness. She didn't want to fight. Why, why had he chosen tonight to do this?

A loud conk sounded. "Aw, baby. You don't need those, do you?" His voice came through, distorted and muffled like he had his face pressed into the other side of the door. "I promise ... I know you're really sensitive ... but I promise your body is the greatest gift I could ever receive. You're the most beautiful woman—"

"Stop," she said loudly and effectively. Kelley couldn't help but press herself further against her side of the door, wishing like hell she didn't have this hang up. "Just stop."

She looked up and stretched her arm as far as it could go along the door, until it was fully extended, and placed it against the wood, still moist from her scalding shower. That's where his boyish, blond waves would be if he was standing straight and tall. She twirled an imaginary, chin length curl in her fingers as they rested against the door, wishing she didn't have to be so mad. But she did.

"Come on, it's the middle of the night. Let me in, I'll wrap you up and carry you back to bed," he said. "It's cold out here without you. And lonely. What do I have to do to get you back under the covers with me?"

Kelley's eyes darted to the ceiling even though she couldn't see much. The cold metal of the doorknob poked her in the belly and she wished his warm arms were something she could accept right now. But taking the chance of him seeing her freakish skin was not going to happen.

If he ever saw, he'd have questions.

She couldn't lie to the man. One look into his eyes and truth poured out of her. Even stupid stuff, especially stupid stuff. What had she told him last night? That she was nervous about their first sleepover and so had spent hours driving up and down his street. Passing his apartments, coming back. Passing, coming back. Finally he'd come out and stood in the freezing cold on the curb and flagged her down. Those deep blue eyes would steal all her secrets.

If there was one thing Kelley would not do to her Jay, it was hurt him by talking about the night she'd been trying to get to him. There wasn't a single thing on this earth that was worth the guilt and horror he'd have to carry around were he to find out she'd been attacked while on her way to see Jay.

"No. No, Jay. Just leave them there." She tried to sound as stern and serious as she could, remembering her mom's tone when corralling Anyell and her for meals when they were kids. "I shouldn't have come over tonight. It's my fault."

She heard another couple of thunks rap against the door. Most likely his big ole, smart noggin' and that unruly hair she could spend hours petting and sinking her fingers through.

"Just like that, angel? We're done? You sure about that?" he asked. His voice was one all his own and it called to every part of her being just then. The memory of all the kind things he whispered to her as they considered taking things further and making love, discreet and covered up love, but still, she never felt more whole than when she was with him and he said things like, "You're so good to me, baby. Let me be good to you."

No, she wasn't sure at all.

"Yes, I'm sure." She wanted to add that he should have known better but denying him and keeping her resolve was already hard enough without baiting him to keep responding to her. His voice called to her to forgive, forget and fall back into his strong arms, his long, muscled body that would keep her covered in the most beautiful darkness two people could share. "I'm not coming out until you promise you've left me something to cover up with."

"Fine, baby. I promise."

It was quiet until a couple minutes later and she could hear him trying the doorknob. No doubt he could get into his own bathroom if he really wanted to. The thought spiked her nerves. "I'm serious, Jay. Please just do it."

"Done," he said. "Wish I knew what exactly it was that has you in there and me out here. Wish you trusted me. I promised you I wouldn't push too hard and that's not my intent."

He knew enough because she'd told him the night of their first date in an effort to scare him off and save him the trouble. "You'll never see me naked." But he'd gotten all wide-eyed and then grinned, swearing he wanted to date her so badly that he'd basically put up with anything she could throw his way. Kelley couldn't help but knee her side of the door.

"Open the door a crack or you're not getting anything," he said in a tone she couldn't quite discern. It wasn't completely playful like usual but if he was mad, he was doing a great job of holding it in.

He was just ornery enough to do it. "Fine," she agreed, "but promise you won't push or try to get in here."

"I promise."

Through the tiny opening she allowed, he passed through her undies and the thin pajama top and bottoms she'd worn. His fingers lingered on the bottoms.

"Thank you," she said when he finally let them go. "I'm just getting dressed and then I'll be out. Jay, I'm gonna go home now."

"No, you're not."

****

Did she really think he was giving up that easily?

Chapter Fourteen

It had been a few hours and she couldn't stand it any longer. Kelley wandered out from Jay's room, layered in her clothes and his blanket, missing him. There he was, on his couch.

"Jay? Please come back to your bed," she poked at him and whispered. Her eyes had adjusted just to the glowing lights of the electronics in his living room. His hips shifted under the sheet he'd tugged out of the linen closet and he sat up and rubbed the balls of his palms over his eyes then through his hair. The movement was sheer intoxication. They'd come so close.

"Hey." He scooted back so she could sit down. "No, I can't."

"What do you mean? No, I'm saying that I want you to come back. I'm over it. I know you didn't mean to do it."

"Babe, that's not the way it works. I pushed too hard, I hurt you and now I'm going to stay here the whole night."

She hated that he was right. "Is this some sort of punishment? Are you trying to get back at me by sleeping out here? For not, not letting you see me?"

He shook his head as if she was the most exasperating person on the face of the planet. "No, no. Of course not. I was just playing tonight but I did something that hurt you. I can't be doing that to you. That's a big deal."

"So you refuse to come back to bed with me?"

"Yeah, I guess that's what I'm saying."

"Are you serious? After the stunt you pulled tonight and the huge deal you made of me staying when I wanted to leave?"

"Yes, babe."

She started to scoot off back to his room alone. But her heart squeezed, stopping her. Inside, the voice that normally told her to keep her distance, not to get close to anyone, actually told her to fight for him.

"Well, can I stay here on the couch with you?"

"Kelley, what's the matter? I'm a big boy, I can handle being on the couch this one night. Trust me, I don't plan to make the same mistake again. Look, I know this sucks, but I'm proud of you. You surprised me by standing your ground. Don't take that back."

He didn't understand. Maybe he never would. How could their relationship last under these circumstances?

The time had come to open up to Jay, no matter how opposed Kelley was to hurting him like she was about to do. News as devastating as this would leave his tender heart crippled. Their roles might finally reverse and she'd be the one he kept out. She'd kept this hidden so long but saw no way past being honest now.

He began speaking before she had the chance to say anything. "Kelley, I can't begin to tell you how overjoyed I am that you stayed the night with me. But it hurts so much now."

He'd caught her off guard with that. She hadn't expected to hear of his pain, having been so focused on her own. She felt horrible. "Why?" she asked.

"The other things I want to do with you in this lifetime." He looked around and rubbed his neck then turned his attention back to her. His words were meant for no one but her, his eyes and his lips told her so as he spoke. "I want to make babies with you someday. Someone will have to see your body. Doctors, nurses. I, I will need to see you naked."

Her courage slipped. How did she look into those blue eyes of his and tell him she'd been seen by others? Both the ones who had damaged her and the ones who'd bandaged her up that night. Physically at least.

Her voice tiptoed past her lips. "They will. I promise."

"*They* will. What about me?" She could tell he didn't want to push her but all other reason and stops had been exhausted between them. The shine in his eyes told her not to do this to him. He was already hurting. This would make it worse. "I need something, baby. I need you to give me *something*," he said. "Otherwise, I don't see how we're gonna make it." Wet and blue, sad eyes pleaded with her.

"That night I never showed up at the club."

"I remember that night. I really just assumed Anyell had convinced you I was a bad idea. I would have agreed with him at that point."

"It had nothing to do with Anyell."

"Okay, so you got cold feet. The club intimidated you and the fact I'm a stripper. It's okay. I got it. I would have been leery of me too. I understand." He caressed her hand.

Swallowing became difficult at best. He wouldn't feel that way once he knew. Finally, she swallowed and heard her throat adjusting in her ears.

"Jay, the reason, that night."

"Babe? What?"

"I was on my way to the club. To see you." She watched his eyes begin to fill with horror and so she scrambled to take it away, to lie if she had to. Anything to spare him this burden. "I decided I was too tired though and would go back home." No, it wasn't true, but she didn't care right now looking into his face.

"What happened?" His weight shifted forward like he was ready to pounce and she was the one dangling something very dangerous in front of him.

"My car broke down on the way."

"On the way to the club or on your way back home? How far away?"

Lying again to save him, she said, "Home. Two blocks, near Vegas and Center."

"That's not a great block." He nearly roared it. "There's more, Kelley. What are you not telling me?"

"Nothing. I decided I wanted to go home. My car broke down when I was on the way back and that's it." She stopped herself from adding the truth, *to you*. Telling Jay he was the reason she'd gotten out of her broken down car and set out on foot, to go to the club and not her house, like an idiot, would drive the knife in even further.

"What aren't you telling me?"

Everything that would hurt him. She shook her head no.

"I didn't see you for an entire year after that. Thought I'd lost you for good," he said, taking her face into his hands. "What. Happened?"

He almost had lost her for good. She remembered being certain she would die. This was going nowhere good. He cared so much for her. And she in turn felt the exact same protectiveness toward him. She'd miss drowning in those blue eyes of his but this had to be done. Jay could never know what those monsters had done to her as she traipsed across the deserted streets, trying her best to get to him. But as she tucked and buried the hurtful truth, still vowing never to speak of it to him, his face blanked. His eyes searched hers like he needed help placing his thoughts but his words had gotten stuck. She understood that feeling so well. Kelley worried whether it was enough that she'd told him she'd decided to head home and not go to the club to see him after all. Would he still take the blame for having her out there in the first place?

"You wear long sleeves and pants when it's 130 degrees outside. You flinch whenever I come near your belly." He blinked. She sucked in a distorted breath. He continued. "What aren't you telling me? Tell me the truth, Kelley." His words should have been punctuated with force but this depraved sounding, hollow voice of his affected her far more deeply. "What happened that night, Kelley? Don't lie to me. Not right now."

"You promised you wouldn't make me talk about this."

"I know," he nearly cried. She heard his voice crack with sorrow. "I know but don't you see? That's not helping you get any better."

She couldn't deny his need to know any longer. Although certain parts would be buried in the grave with her. "Three guys. One me." The skin between her eyes began to quiver as she fought not to fall and surrender to the ground.

"Oh God, baby." Immediately his arms were wrapped around her in a vice.

"I thought I could make it home in one piece," she said, her only thought being the one to shield him from the truth. "I was wrong. I'm sorry I've made this so hard between us, but I, there are just parts of me I don't want you to see."

That was as much truth as she was willing to give him. She loved him, she'd known that for some time now, but the look in his eyes said she was about to lose him for good.

****

Jay's mind spun as he fought not to punch holes in the wall. What had been done to her? What had he let happen? "I should have driven you that night myself. I failed you. This is my fault."

"No. There is nothing you could have done to stop it."

The words came out of her mouth and he knew in his heart that she believed them. What had they done to make her wince at his touch for the next … dang, she still did it every once in a while, he realized, and it had been over a year now. The long sleeves she'd worn had been so out of place and he'd chosen to ignore it for his own comfort. He was a bastard.

"You had bruises you were trying to hide?" he guessed, seeing dark blood shades of red creep up in his vision.

She nodded, finally after some time had passed.

"They hit you?" God, please let her say no but what left a bruise? Something pretty powerful and painful. "With their hands?"

"No," she said so quietly. Foolishly, his heart lightened for a second until he realized what that meant. If their fists hadn't done it, that meant something else had. "Not their hands, no hitting," she barely let out.

He was going to lose it if everything he imagined kept getting trumped by the truth she was telling. He gritted his teeth and closed his eyes tight, preparing for her to again tell him his guess was far kinder than reality.

"Did they cut you?" he hated to ask but remembered seeing a slashing scar sticking out from her sleeve one day while they'd walked a few weeks ago. "Was that what happened? Why you wear long sleeves in August in 130-degree weather?"

She nodded yes. Oh hell. Jay felt his blood pressure skyrocket throughout every vein in his system. They'd cut her? Those monsters. He'd kill them with his bare hands. He'd do it right now. His head pounded and he could have cried at what had been done to her on a night she should have been with him. Safe, with him. Like she was now except for she looked terrified with her searching eyes and the way she looked to be holding her guts in. He pulled her to his chest, vowing never to let go.

"Oh baby, knife wounds?"

A moment passed. He'd been holding her so tight but she'd kept her face tilted up so he could see her. God, here she was being so brave, even after he'd acted like such an ass by stealing her clothes. But then after he planted a kiss on her forehead, she stopped looking him in the eyes and that was when he sensed something unimaginable was about to come. His stomach became nauseous. He waited while she blinked.

"Bite marks," she said.

He was right.

His heart sank as they stood there staring at each other.

Bite marks.

He shouldn't have said it, but he couldn't think straight. "Let me see."

Her answer shouldn't have surprised him, yet it always did.

"No," she said before touching a trembling hand to his cheek for a split second and then turning around and leaving his room.

He waited to hear the sound of her turning on the TV in the living room or the opening and closing of the refrigerator. But none of those things happened. He panicked and went after her, forgetting the vow to wait and take a few minutes so his anger for the assholes didn't get projected onto Kelley. When he found Kelley a few seconds later, she had her hand on the door knob to the front door of his house and her overnight bag hung from her shoulder. Her hair was still messy from having had his hands in it.

"Don't go, Kelley."

"Please don't make this any harder than it already is," she said.

"Look, this is what I know. I want you to stay and I want you to trust me and tell me what happened. I want us to work through this together." He felt as baffled as she must look. "If you didn't trust me, you wouldn't have come over here tonight." He went to her, removed her hand from the doorknob and held it and kissed it. "We've gotta work through this together. I want you and I need you, baby."

He had no idea how she would respond to that.

****

Kelley had no idea what to say to him. She'd said as much as she could and knew they'd moved beyond the talking. He needed sharing at this point. He'd all but begged her to trust him and let him see what had been done. He knew now that she had bite marks but when he saw them, it would be different.

God, she loved him so much, too much. Her need was completely irrational, she knew it and she knew it would snatch him away from her.

He pulled her to him and spoke into her hair.

"What was it? Dogs? God, tell me some sadistic pricks didn't set their dogs loose on you." She heard his voice hitch and his chin and lips pressing tightly onto the top of her head.

Her angel had no idea.

Jay took her hand and started to pull up on her sleeve. She froze. Her response should have been to jerk her hand away but she just froze.

****

Jay pulled slowly at her shirt, first just the sleeves, testing her. Oddly, she let him. Her arms at the hands and wrists were clear but once he looked up to the bend of her elbow, the place where most people got blood drawn, he saw the beginnings of tiny silvery white scars.

What the?

Desperate to let her know she was safe with him and that he was reacting not because he found her scars hideous but because he found what those monsters had done to her repulsive, he made sure to look her directly in her eyes as he found the material of her shirt and for a second, debated. He wouldn't pull it up. Fear spiked in her eyes and it was so real that he knew this was no game. This also was not the time to hurt her in anyway. He ran the tips of his fingers gently over the skin of her midsection but left the shirt hanging. He felt the lumps and ridges. So many of them.

He could feel his eyes searching hers. Every movement they made. He tried so hard not to let his eyes become affected by what he was feeling with his hands but it was impossible. After only a few seconds, and almost involuntarily, Jay brought his hand up to his mouth in a fist and just held it there. If he let his fist fall, there would be nothing keeping his emotions jammed inside.

Kelley's lips stayed pulled in tightly, her teeth holding them closed from the inside as they stared at each other. Maybe he did need to see. Here she was being so brave for him, he'd damned well better be the stronger one. With the lightest touch he could manage, he pulled her shirt up and finally saw what he'd just run his fingers over.

Jay couldn't believe what his brain was trying to tell him. "They bit you. Those assholes, *they* bit you." No wonder she was so scared to let him in. Finally, he understood. He would never go back on his promise and ask her for more than she could give again. Even if it took years, he would wait. He would be patient. He would be whatever it took, whatever she needed. There was no question now. He loved her unconditionally and knew with every ounce of conviction he had that his job on this earth was to protect and take care of her, not push her into doing something she wasn't ready for. Jay pulled her to him once he felt her start to relax.

"I'm sorry, my sweet angel." Tears ran down the back of his throat and he'd give anything for a rewind button, to not have tormented her with his prank tonight. God how he wished he could take that back.

But he did want her to know one thing.

Each movement he made now was slower because he wanted her to have the time to react to everything he did. "You have never been more beautiful to me than you are right now. Your bravery and strength take my breath away. I don't know what I would do if I lost you because of my stupidity. Actually, yes I do know. It would kill me, Kelley. Please forgive me for pushing you beyond your limits tonight. Sex is just a physical act and someday yes, I want to make love with you, I want to be intimate with you, but I don't need that, and if you can't, I'll happily go without if it means hurting you. But know how proud I am of you for opening up and letting me see. You are my hero, Kell."

Kelley pulled out of his embrace, surprising him.

"Where are you going?" he asked.

****

She didn't know. To the kitchen? Maybe back into the shower. He could deny it all he wanted but Kelley knew her sweet man was a sexual creature by nature. It was one of the most beautiful parts of his spirit.

She was as equally fascinated by that as she was intimidated.

He hadn't flinched not once just now at seeing her scars.

She'd spent all this time terrified she'd lose him if he ever set eyes on them and in mere seconds, he'd erased all that self-doubt and judgment that had ruled her for too long. She'd thought that she needed to heal herself and get past the trauma of her past before she could really be his fully but now realized that she needed his help. That it was okay to ask. Even more okay to accept.

He was willing to go without the physical love they both craved.

Well, she was not.

The time had come to trust. The time had come to believe in the goodness of human beings again. The time had come to love Jay like he deserved, with everything she had. No holding back. If she couldn't do that, then she didn't deserve him and should let him go.

"I'm done letting the bad stuff keep me from the good guy, Jay."

Kelley looked over his shoulder toward his door and made her way around him where he stood planted. She walked until her back was up against the front door of his apartment. She didn't care what was on the other side. What was going on out there was irrelevant because she knew that with him by her side and in her heart, everything would be okay. No, not okay, but wonderful. The best.

She looked at him now and let what she was feeling in her heart, in her body, bubble up to her face. Something special fixed itself in her gaze which locked onto Jay's. She could feel his energy change as he saw her changing her outlook right before his eyes. All the times he'd made her feel so incredibly desirable, just by the look in his eyes. That was the effect she was now having on him and she loved it.

"You don't have to do this, Kelley."

At that, she hooked her thumbs into her pajama bottoms and pushed them down until they fell to the floor. Fire caught in his gaze.

"What are you doing, angel?"

She pulled up her top and let it fall to the ground next. Caution mixed with the fire and she had to admit, she could not read Jay in this moment. The confusion stopped her striptease. She searched his eyes and in less than a second, he moved to her and took her body into his in a tight embrace. It felt wonderful pressing up against his bare chest like this, feeling him breathe and expand. Having this strong of an effect on someone she regarded so highly, it did things to her that she couldn't explain. She let out a deep breath of her own as his face nuzzled against her cheek. He then cupped the sides of her face in his tender hands.

"I just want to look at you," he said. His voice melted away the last of her fears and inhibitions. "Just, just let me look at you, angel."

She nodded, accepting that this was his need in this moment and a warmth filled her entire being that she possessed the ability to provide it for him. His blue eyes roamed the length of her body, her face, even her toes. And then as she remained standing, he dropped to his knees and laid the side of his head against her stomach.

"You know I am fully committed to you Kelley, don't you?" His lips moved against her belly.

"Yes." Where was he going with this? Her fingers caressed their way through his hair. He had such nice hair and a fantasy of him letting her wash it shocked her to her core. She smiled at her change of heart and the secret thoughts of them sharing his shower now. He hadn't seen her blush but that was okay.

"You know that work is just work. You know I have a great time there but it's my job."

"Yes, and the fact you're so good at it makes me proud. I love the fact that you're a nightly smile on the ladies' faces."

She felt his head pulling back just enough so he could look up into her eyes. Something about the clarity in his eyes made her entire being tingle.

"Kelley Phillips, that right there is why I would be so honored if you would be my partner in life. Will you marry me?"

"Can we do it tonight?" she asked, suddenly eager.

"Hahaha, well it is my day off. So sure! Wait, are you asking to get married tonight or to do it, like doing the nasty?"

"Jay!" He never stopped with the jokes.

"Because I've decided I'm going to wait until you're Mrs. Jaymes Henriksen to make love to you. I will always do right by you. You are the most precious treasure in the world to me. I may screw up. You know I'm not the tidiest guy on the planet. But I will never fail you."

That was all she needed to hear. "Then I'm asking to get married tonight."

He bit the side of his bottom lip and she touched it as he did it with the pad of her finger. He stood to his full height and lifted her up in his arms then walked her over to the kitchen counter where he sat her down.

"Don't be shy now," he said and wrapped her legs around his waist. "How did I get so lucky, huh?" he asked.

"I think patience worked in both our favors. Make no mistake about it, Jay. I'm the lucky one."

"I don't know about that," he said, shaking his head and then squeezed her bottom and pulled her completely into him. He'd always taken care not to do that. Feeling his arousal for the first time as it pressed into her sent her body into a frenzy. She squeezed her thighs tighter around his waist which made him chuckle. "Tonight though, I do intend to make you feel like not just the luckiest girl in the world, but the sexiest, most beautiful, and most cherished."

"Then the joke is finally on you, Jay. Because you've already done that. A million times over."

They stayed there in his kitchen with her on the counter and him standing between her legs for a long time, just swaying to the feeling of absolute love between them, wrapped up in each other and waiting for the night to fall.

Kelley had a surprise planned for Jay tonight. She had a feeling he would be a very happy man on their wedding night.

Chapter Fifteen

October 1ˢᵗ, 2015. My wedding night. Hell yeah!

I bet you didn't think it was ever gonna happen, right? No worries, I had my doubts too. But we did it. I still can't believe it. So, first order of business while Kell is in the bathroom doing her girly stuff, the setting right now. Hmm, what I can tell you is that there's a good reason people flock to Vegas to get married. Our hotel is the bomb. One stop shop, I'm not kidding. Wedding chapel? Check. Room service? Oh yeah. Killer swimming pool? Are you kidding me? The thing looks just like one of those private island getaways I know you ladies like to fantasize about on Pinterest.

And I splurged for Mrs. Henriksen. (If there are any guys out there reading this, *spring* for the best when it comes to your lady. Bros!) Our honeymoon suite consists of a king-sized bed and a private hot tub. Yeah, there's a few other things in here but huge bed, huge hot tub. That's my brain on wedding night. I'm totally fist bumping you all right now. Man, if you could see the smile on my face.

Oh, I think I just heard my *wife* turning the water off. I have a few candles to light. Ladies, this is what it's all about. You are so very worth this, not just on the wedding night, but every night. If your man, or woman, whoever it is you love and are sharing yourself with, if that person isn't treating you like the treasure you are, tell them Jay said it's never too late to start, or hey, you go find somebody who's willing to be everything you want and need. Most importantly, stop questioning whether you're worth it. You are. And if you still have your doubts, you come see me at the club. I'll remind ya.

(winky emoji). So help a guy out? What song should I have playing when the wifey comes out of the bathroom? Yeah, I agree. After all, that's kind of our song. Hey, thanks for letting me hijack the one liner setting teaser again. Haha! Guess I'm just more suited to going big rather than small. I hope your minds all just took a quick dip into the gutter with me. All right then, back to the story. Ladies, have fun. Be yourselves. I promise, you'll be at your most beautiful when you do. And if no one else sees that, don't worry. Just open your eyes and see for yourselves. Smile, the best is yet to come.

****

October 1ˢᵗ, 2015. A sweet little hotel in North Vegas where it was 'bout to get hot…

"Jay! Jay!"

Kelley screamed like she was stuck in the bathroom with whatever it was that made women scream like girls. Jay may as well have donned a cape as he prepared to perform his first official duty as a husband. A rescue. "Man, I hope it's small if it's a spider," he whispered so that only he could hear. There were two things guys really didn't like but turned the other cheek to in the name of chivalry. Large, scary spiders and getting slapped when they said or did the wrong thing. He made his way to the bathroom door after cueing up "Where You Belong" by his *wife's* first love. On the way, he walked past the small table where two candles he'd found at the gift shop burned. Sugar cookies and candy corn scented their room. He hoped she liked it. The sweetness was way overpowering to his senses but Jay didn't sweat the small stuff anymore. Kelley was a constant reminder of that for him. For that, he was eternally grateful.

If she could let go of a painful past, anyone could, including him.

"Yes, dear," he called out, chuckling to himself.

But as soon as he opened the door, he was thunderstruck.

Standing before him, she absolutely glowed.

Just like the angel she was. With her thick hair pulled up in a messy bun on top of her head and pieces falling everywhere, she stood there wearing his white wedding shirt and his black tie. She swam in it, of course, which made it all the sexier.

He had to clear his throat. He watched her gaze drop down to the crotch of his suit pants and he did good to keep himself from moaning at the curiosity painted all over her face. That, her body language, and knowing this would be her first time making love all had him rock hard. Jay didn't want to hide that from Kelley but he also didn't want to overwhelm her. The pull was magnetic. She called to him and he came, unable to stop from pulling her into his body. God, she fit so perfectly. He loved that he had to lean down to kiss her forehead. When she didn't shy away from his arousal, his heart swelled.

"Do you like my outfit?" she asked.

"Immensely. I'd love to find out what you've got underneath there." He gave her a flirty wink which made the tips of her ears turn rosy.

"Maybe I stole your boxers, too," she said with the cutest attempt at flirty seduction he'd ever witnessed and couldn't help but tease her back.

"Tsk tsk tsk, Mrs. Henriksen. We both know better than that, being that I didn't bring any."

Her eyes went double their size. God, he loved that.

The silhouette of her body, those sexy little curves he'd waited so long to taste, showed through against the white cotton each time she squirmed but for now, he stayed where he was, fighting the urge to make love to her where she stood.

"Stop squirming, wifey." He wouldn't warn her again. Jay had been patient for so long and tonight was about satisfying their mutual hunger, not holding back. Her first time was going to be amazing. A night he'd try to top every night for the rest of their lives. He wanted to set the bar high. "Turn around, I want the full view," he said softly, trying out a tender command, and waited for her blush to fade before he turned her like a sexy ballerina. She went up on her tiptoes, flexing her calf muscles as he spun her in a slow circle. His mouth watered and he couldn't help himself, becoming even harder. Jay picked her up and tossed her over his shoulder to take her out to the bed but when he turned toward the bathroom door, he caught a glimpse of her bare ass in the mirror. He stopped to enjoy the surprise for a moment. The back view of beautiful pink flesh centered perfectly between her cheeks and thighs and set off by a soft covering of short, dark hair, on full display for him, glistened under the dim lights.

"Jay?" she asked in a quiet voice that let him know she was probably nervous and his having stalled might not be helping.

"Sorry." But he wasn't really. And, he wanted her to see what they did to each other. So he went ahead and set her down. "I want you to see something."

"Okay. I have a feeling you may have just seen one of my surprises for you. You were right, no boxers."

"I may have." He grinned and unbuttoned his pants. As soon as he did, her gaze fell to his fingers. "It was beautiful. I liked it very much," he said, about to show her exactly how much.

"Really? Well good."

"You're so silly, Kell. Of course I loved seeing that part of you. I love seeing every part of you. Come here."

She turned to him and he once again lifted her up but this time he set her back down on the vanity and then finished undoing his pants. He could tell she wasn't sure where to look. "You can and should watch what I'm doing. I like it very much when you watch me."

"Okay," she said shyly. By tonight, they'd be doing things that left no room for blushing and uncertainty.

Jay looked her in the eyes and then used her chin to lower Kelley's gaze. He knew when he had the right spot because her eyes widened before she blinked several times. He had his pants open now, hanging there showing her that he'd also foregone underwear. "I guess we had the same idea." That got a smile out of her. "Keep watching," he told her and slowly inched his pants down, revealing more of his skin to her little by little, putting to use some of his expert stripping skills. She gasped when he stopped where he did, allowing his butt and erection to be the only things holding his pants up. "You like?"

"Yes," she said just barely and blinked some more. Her lips parted as she watched him, clearly fascinated by his movements.

Jay knew it was time to touch himself so that she would feel comfortable doing it too. His hand went to his cock that was still covered with his pants. With a small smile, he slid his pants away from his erection and let them fall to a pile at his feet. He returned his hand to his head and spread the moisture leaking from the tip into the rest of him with his thumb. "How do you feel watching me do this?" he asked her.

"Um, what do you mean?"

"I mean, what is your body feeling right now? Do you feel it in your stomach? Between your thighs?" He also leaned in and kissed her nose and then her lips, just small pecks for now. Lastly, he used the fingertip of his free hand to touch the skin right around her clit. She shuddered but smiled.

"Yes," she said. He smiled too.

"Yes, you're feeling all of that, in all those places?" She didn't have to answer. He could tell by her face and the way her eyes had locked with his. The way her lips had parted and how she was rolling her upper body forward into each breath she took. She was experiencing this wonderful pleasure for the very first time and it was being done at his hand. "You are so beautiful."

Jay continued stroking himself from shaft to tip a few more times as she returned to watching him but then he was ready for the next part. She might not be ready to practice on herself yet so he decided they would keep using him as their example. He centered her on the bathroom vanity and spread her thighs with his hands, leaving her in his white shirt for now. Completely naked now and feeling super fantastic, he stepped into the space he'd just made and took her hands in his then kissed her palms. He placed them on his shoulders and felt how sweaty they were. He couldn't help but grin at that and gave them one more round of kisses. "It's okay," he whispered to her. "I'm nervous, too."

"You are?" she asked, sounding like she doubted that.

"Yes, but only a little." Slowly he guided her hands from his shoulders down over his chest. He wanted to make sure she got the chance to feel it all, in depth and enjoy it. He planned to do the same when it was his turn to touch her. Once he was sure she was getting pleasure from having his flesh and muscles under her hands, he drew them downward, passing over his pecs and abs. At his hips, he let her hands go to see if she wanted to explore on her own.

Her hands stayed where he left them.

"Jay?"

"Yeah, babe?"

"Don't let go. Not yet."

God, she was so precious to him. Jay took her two hands back in his and ran them along his hip muscles, travelling downward along his vee and then trailed them around to his backside where he deposited them on his ass cheeks. "Hold these," he said with a grin.

"Okay," she said and even gave his buns a squeeze.

"Oh God, yes. Perfect."

He cleared a few pieces of her fallen hair out from her eyes. "You look so beautiful, Kelley. I need you to promise me you'll never doubt that. I am so proud of how far you've come. I remember that extremely young woman I met last year. I was so impressed by you then but I look at you now. You absolutely blow my mind. You're such an inspiration to me. God, thank you so much for coming back. Time and time again."

She didn't respond, other than to lay the perfect kiss on his lips. Her taste sent him to heaven as he worked her mouth with his, getting completely lost in the passion exploding between them. It was just natural that his hands started roaming her body from her delicate shoulders down to her hips. He wanted this shirt off of her so he could feel her skin.

He was treated to a nibble by her teeth on his upper lip and it drove his desire to insane levels. "Trust me," he said into her mouth as he also touched his tongue with hers in their delicious play.

"I do."

Not breaking their hot kiss, he grabbed the shirt and ripped it open, sending buttons flying in all directions. She gasped inside his mouth.

"Doing okay?" he asked, pulling back so he could read her expression. It was difficult because the same passion he was sure had swallowed him whole had her as well. She nodded and he kept his eyes on her while his hands instinctively went to her breasts. They filled his hands perfectly and felt so warm and soft. With his hands on her chest, his thumbs playing circles across her nipples which he thought were very nice, he felt her holding her breath. "Kelley? You gotta breathe, babe. You know I'm in heaven. I'm loving this. And you're doing so great. I'm so proud of you."

She swallowed again. "You haven't looked yet."

She was wrong, he'd stared at her until he memorized the beauty and uniqueness that was Kelley that first night she'd shown herself to him. Her scars didn't bother him, only that he knew she'd suffered so horribly receiving them. But the scars themselves were a part of her and he loved every part of her.

"That's because I love watching your face reacting to my touch. I can't begin to explain the pleasure that gives me. Every gasp you make, every time your lips fall apart because my fingers are playing with you or squeezing you or exploring deep inside you. When you bite down. Oh my God, Kelley. I'm practically exploding over here, babe."

Maybe there was only one way to show her what he was trying to say. He decided to take his kiss down to the skin he knew she worried so deeply about. "Close your eyes," he told her. "Do you like the feel of my hands here?" he asked as he stroked and petted her shoulders and then worked his way down to her breasts again and then her rib cage. Immediately, she started exhibiting all the signs he'd just told her he loved.

"Mm-hmm," she purred.

"Okay, how about now?"

Jay softly but confidently felt his way over her abdomen, not wanting her to think he was tiptoeing around the area. He wasn't ashamed of her and his touch should reflect that. "You're so beautiful, Kelley. I could touch you here for days."

She didn't respond this time but he sensed she enjoyed his being so affirmative with her. Her breathing was even and her face relaxed. It was then that he nuzzled his nose and mouth between her breasts and slid down, leaving kisses as he went down the center of her ribs, straight to her belly button. He made sure to massage with his hands at the same time as he was delivering his kisses. He wanted her so mind to be filled with physical senses so that there was no room for insecurities and fear.

There was one scar that was worse than the others and inside, he cried for his wife and the torture she'd endured. Outwardly, he paid special attention to the area, wanting to begin a new series of memories for her to have where it was concerned. For many minutes, he licked and suckled and kissed Kelley's tummy.

Satisfied beyond belief that she'd just allowed him to do that, Jay wanted desperately to get back to another task at hand. Showing her the other telltale signs her body gave off that she craved him the same way he craved her. "Your skin tastes amazing, by the way. Come here. Turn around for me," he instructed her with love and reverence in his voice.

Jay stayed standing, giving his chest as a backrest for Kelley as he placed his hands solidly on her hips and turned her. She remained sitting on her butt on the vanity and together, they looked into the mirror, watching themselves. He had to give it to her, she was one brave, tough cookie.

She gasped but her forehead crinkled.

"Kelley, look at yourself. See what I see. There is no one more wonderful, special, beautiful and sexy than you. Every single part of you. See that." He'd keep telling her, day after day, until she saw it too. She blinked but opened her eyes and took a few minutes just studying her scars. After a bit, Jay began caressing her stomach again, being sure to touch all of the skin there, the rigid parts with the scars and the smooth ones without, as Kelley watched. They would get there. Slowly but surely, he'd never give up convincing her. But right now, there was something else he had to point out to his virgin wife. Damn, every time he thought of being her first, his body and heart fired and sparked.

"Open your legs for me," he said, maintaining the controlled calm over the fire he felt.

"Okay," she complied. Her knees parted only half a foot.

"More please." He didn't know how better to instruct her so he went ahead and took her by the knees and pushed them outward, opening her like a beautiful flower.

"Look at you. God, Kelley."

"You've said that a lot tonight." She said it and then let her head dip to the side, resting against his arm which he used to cradle her. "I like it."

"Tell me if you like this." Jay kissed the top of her head and his hands used her inner thighs as slopes to glide down and end at her womanly perfection. First he petted her opening and the soft hairs using all his fingers and thumb and then slowly, he switched to just one finger, opening up her folds. As soon as he did that, the shiny gloss that coated her kicked his own body into extreme overdrive. His stomach clenched as he felt himself tightening and that ticklish feeling swirling in his stomach became almost unbearable. He'd have to have her soon. His control was pretty damn good but this was the most turned on he'd ever been.

"See how this area right here glistens, Kelley?"

She nodded a yes.

"That's your body telling me you want me. That you're ready to take me inside of you." He rubbed the slit up and down with just his thumb, switching between coarse strokes and soft ones. She gasped the gasp he loved. "What does your heart say? What does your head tell you, my love? Are we all in agreement?" He nuzzled her cheek as she watched with an innocent yet raw hunger painted all over her face.

"I want to learn to read you like that."

"Oh sweetheart, I'm so easy." He nearly chuckled but could see in her eyes that she was very serious. "You're going to get sick and tired of me walking around with a hard on all the time."

She dipped her head to the side again. He knew it was due to her still getting used to the knowledge now that she indeed affected him so strongly. "I will never get tired of that. But I meant the way you read me earlier. My expressions. What are yours? How will I know if you are really enjoying what I'm doing with you? After you teach me all the things it is that you like first. I'm sorry, I wish I knew more for you."

"Angel, I look forward, seriously, to dangerous extremes, I look forward to being your teacher in all this stuff. You really do have the advantage here, though. We guys, we're just open books when it comes to being turned on. If I'm looking at you and you're in the room with me, you can assume I'm enjoying you. Whether we're touching or on opposite sides of the room. I'm *always* going to welcome your touch. I'm *always* going to want you. Does that help?"

"I think so. Yes. Will I always want you, too? Am I also that easy?"

"Hmm, good questions." He kissed her and used this moment while they chatted to rub his hands over her skin starting at her feet and ending at her shoulders and then going again. He loved massaging her. "I like to think that in theory, you will always want me. But you'll probably have days when you're just not in the mood. And that's totally okay. You just have to tell me if I'm being dense that day and not picking up on it."

"Okay. Jay?"

"Yeah babe?" he asked and made a pass up the outsides of her toned thighs. He found a couple new ridges that he knew instantly were more scars but made sure not to react. He just kept right on with his caressing.

"I want you now," she said.

****

"I want you now too," he echoed back into her ear, licking and nibbling around the tender edge which made her squirm.

"Jay, I bet if you looked now, you'd see that I'm super turned on."

"I can't believe you just had the balls to say that. I'm so proud of you. I just never know what's going to come out of this sexy mouth! I love it. Come here."

Kelley only had seconds before Jay scooped her up again, tossed her over his shoulder like it was nothing, and took her from the bathroom to the giant bed. "You're so strong."

The view of his bared backside as she rode over his shoulder was amazing. The man had the sweetest bubble butt. She gave it a playful swat which got her one in return. "Hey now," he said, "that's gonna get you in lots of trouble."

He then laid her down with so much care that she felt just like a rose. It was hard enough remembering to breathe, let alone imagining Jay's beautifully perfect and muscled body fitting inside hers but she'd wanted that exact experience with him for a long time now. Longer than he realized.

He pushed her down into the wonderfully plush mattress. As he did so, his shoulders flexed. Her heart sped up. How was it that this man was all hers? With all the heightened sensations currently owning her body, how had they gone this long without making love?

"What are you thinking?" he asked as he held her face in his hands as he was apt to do. She loved the amount of time her face spent in those capable hands of his.

"I have a bone to pick with you."

"Oh yeah? I have a bone for you too," he said and grabbed his crotch as he sat straddling over top of her.

"Jay!" But really, his humor was hands down the sexiest thing about him and his joking was the only thing keeping her from having an anxiety attack right now. She was so nervous because he was so sexy and so experienced. And so comfortable in his own skin. "Teach me how to be more like you," she couldn't help but say, allowing her thoughts to form into spoken words.

He became very serious then and laid his large body over top of her. His weight was a lot to bear but she found that she loved it. It came as a huge surprise, but he actually turned his head away so that she couldn't see him.

"Jay, what's wrong? What did I say? Please look at me."

Kelley reached up and held his hand until he did as she asked.

"I can't tell you how much what you just said means to me. I'm sorry, it just got to me."

"Now you're gonna make me cry," she said and pulled on his shoulders, signaling that she needed to hold him and be held.

"Yeah, we seriously need to get to the good stuff."

"I love you, Jay."

"I love you too, Kelley. Now where was I?"

"Hmm. We were talking about bones."

At that, he cracked up laughing so loudly, she was sure the entire hotel would hear. "You are mine. I will not share. Ever. Unless you're secretly into that and even then, it's gonna be really hard but I'd do anything for you." Even though he was being playful, she saw the intensity behind his stare. The depth of his eyes and the beauty in his lips. It was only another second before she felt his hands roaming every inch of her skin again and the best surprise? She didn't want him to stop. Ever.

Her man was a master at the fine art of touching. Lost in the pleasure building between her thighs, Kelley closed her eyes and allowed herself to just feel.

When she did that, everything became even more intense and superb.

His lips were at her throat, his tongue teased her relentlessly. Lean hips lined with the perfect amount of muscle pressed and grinded against her thigh as he seemed to be everywhere all at once. She loved that he was that much longer than her and could easily stimulate her from top to bottom without having to leave either area. "Jay, I'm feeling it so much right now. I think I need you inside me." She had no idea where the courage came to be that honest with him but it hadn't even taken her a second thought. She felt like she could tell him anything.

"I'm ready too, sweetheart."

For the first time tonight, she realized he had lit candles and music played softly in the background. "Is that The Weeknd?" she asked.

"The one and only. For my girl."

With that, he stopped all possibility of her talking anymore. Her mouth was full with his playful tongue and demanding kiss. His fingers were fisted in her hair, one at the back of her head and one at the side. She could feel him spreading her legs further apart with just the force of his strong knees and thighs. His hands might be preoccupied but hers were not and she used them to squeeze and rub up and down the muscles of those thighs. Dancer's thighs, she thought and beamed inside with so much pride. With his mouth now at her ear, she could hear his breath hitch and every other one or so, he moaned. He didn't have to tell her. He was preparing to enter her. Her entire body broke out in warm flashes and goose bumps. She reached up and around as best she could and pulled him downward, having no shame in the desperate way she wanted him. She shouldn't have to use words either. Let him feel how much she needed this connection to him.

Something warm and incredibly hard pressed up against her and she knew it was time.

"Take a breath, angel," he instructed.

She did as he said. On the inhale, she felt him slide inside her. She let out a loud ahh.

"I know, baby, me too," he said. "Me too."

Jay's body was inside hers. It was a wonderful miracle and that ticklish ball she'd been feeling all night in her belly and between her thighs had grown in intensity. Jay began thrusting himself, rocking his pelvis against hers. He had to be in so deep for that to be possible.

"Are you okay?" he asked.

"Of course," was all she could get out.

Their panting rose together as did their moans.

She loved what he asked of her next. "Scream my name out loud, angel."

"Jay! Jay, I love this! I love you so much. God this feels so amazing!" She didn't care who heard.

She'd screamed the entire thing and his response was to speed up and drive in deeper.

That ball she'd been feeling was about to erupt. "Jay, I, I think—"

"Okay baby, don't think. Just feel it. Let it take you over."

She relaxed into the swirling and then it happened. She had her first orgasm.

It felt amazing.

But not as amazing as what happened next.

Jay's body loved her. She knew because he looked at her just before his body exploded inside hers, and it was a brand new look.

"Oh God. Oh. Oh."

If she didn't know better, she'd say her man was slightly speechless. She knew the feeling.

The moisture of his seed spilling from inside her as he pulled out was inexplicably wonderful. He was wonderful. Their life together was going to be nothing short of heaven because she planned to make each day count.

Jay lay with his head resting on her chest. "I can hear your heart beating," he said.

"My heart is beating because I had to make it back to you, Jay. Thank you for being so patient and never giving up. I'm going to make each day of the rest of your life spectacular. Starting with the rest of tonight. I have one more surprise for you."

****

Whatever it was, "Yes, please," was his answer.

He'd never come that much and never, ever had he come inside a woman without a condom. It was hot and he was ready for this surprise.

Jay sat up on their bed and watched her as she slinked down off the mattress. Totally naked, totally his. She disappeared into the bathroom for a moment and when she reappeared, she had a towel wrapped around her under her arms. She tossed him a towel too.

"Are you still in your birthday suit under there, Mrs. Henriksen?"

"Yes, sir," she said back and the sir part stirred his passion like never before. He'd fallen in love with bondage and the role playing that came along with his dom/sub act at the club. One of these days, he'd teach her more about that world. For now, he had to know what that devilish look turning her fifty shades of sexy meant.

"Come on, handsome husband of mine. This involves swimming."

"You mean skinny dipping, don't you?"

"Yes, sir."

Okay, she was going to have to stop saying that or he was going to tie her up and spank her until she begged him to stop. Soft swats and probably with a feather of course because he'd never hurt her.

"Well, are you coming?" she asked with the most provocative come hither look he'd ever seen.

"Let me see … um, yes," he said with lots and lots of enthusiasm. "Now, tomorrow, forever. Let's go get our skinny dipping on. How fun!"

"You're like a little kid right now. I love you, Jay."

"I love you too, angel. Forever."

The End

****

The End? That's kind of depressing. I'm not ready to let you go! I didn't even get to tell you the most important part of the story yet. The thing you've been dying to know...

Yep, our kids finally got their names. It came down to a heated match of rock, paper, scissors that I totally won. Hey, not my fault Kelley can't concentrate when I'm in my pj's. (winky emoji). So, the most awesome kitty in the world is named ... Mr. Mistoffelees, for obvious reasons. Totally cool, right? Yeah, he could care less. He's not impressed by his namesake or the fact we've watched his magical song video 347 times on YouTube. No, he's way more interested in curling up in my special undies drawer and shedding. Don't laugh. You haven't lived until you've shown up at work and your locker is stuffed with lint rollers. Pocket-sized ones, at that. Good times. And his partner in crime? That crazy little ball of puppy energy who still loves to lick? Well, that one was easy. She's our Angel.

Okay, I guess I feel better saying goodbye now, but The End just feels so final. How about this instead? Smile and be patient because good things come to those who don't give up, and I'll see you next time...

www.carlenelove.com

Evernight Publishing

www.evernightpublishing.com